WE CARRY ON

TALES OF THE WAR

BY

A. TOLSTOY
M. SHOLOKHOV
V. KATAYEV
K. SIMONOV
S. SERGEYEV-TSENSKI
N. TIKHONOV
L. SOBOLEV
V. KOZHEVNIKOV
E. PETROV
B. LAVRENEV
V. LIDIN
P. PAVLENKO
F. PANFEROV
I. EHRENBOURG

Fredonia Books
Amsterdam, The Netherlands

We Carry On:
Tales of the War

by
Alexei Tolstoy
Mikhail Sholokhov
Ilya Ehrenbourg
et al.

ISBN: 1-4101-0688-8

Reprinted from the 1942 edition

Fredonia Books
Amsterdam, The Netherlands
http://www.fredoniabooks.com

CONTENTS

Daredevils

THIS WAS in the northwestern direction. . . .
We were lying stretched out on the sweet-smelling
grass, in a dense hazel grove. The signaller's post was
well concealed; the sky, a pallid-blue from the sultry
heat, was empty. It was so hot that one could almost
hear the leaves crackle. Somewhere nearby was an ant-
hill and Lieutenant Zhabin, every now and then, brushed
an ant from his cheek. Chewing a stalk of grass he was
in no hurry to begin his narrative.

"The German soldier is forbidden to use his brains,
it's a function that's considered harmful amongst the fascists," he said, "his brain-pan is not adapted to grasp-
ing things at a glance—why, by the time he wakes
up. . . . Well, it was just these seconds that enabled us
to pull through. . . . We were in a pretty bad hole—
there's no doubt about that. Looking back at things now—
why, the very thought is enough to make a cold shiver
run down your spine. . . . Our men, of course, are plucky
chaps. Take signaller Petrov—why, judging by his looks,
nobody would ever say that he was such a daring chap.
He's too good looking for a man—dreamy eyes, a sort of
mist in them—he sends his girl a postcard every day. . . .
The men are always having a dig at him: 'Petrov, what
are you—flesh and blood or a walking dummy? You're
at the front, man—wake up. . . .' 'Chuck it, you fellows,'
he would reply, 'nobody'll catch me napping in an emergency. . . .' "

"Comrade Zhabin, but how did you manage to roam around with twenty-five Red Armymen for so many days behind the fascist lines and come through without a scratch?" asked the man with a notebook on his knees.

Zhabin turned over on his side:

"I have a chauffeur who's real smart. I asked him once: 'Whatever made you take to fiddling around with a wheel, Shmelkov? You should have been at a university, in the physics and mathematical faculty....' 'Just happened,' he replied, 'sort of slipped into the job when I was still a kid....' You want to know how we got stranded behind the German lines? Well, you see, I was ordered to concentrate all our equipment in the village of 'P' and maintain contact with staff headquarters until the very last minute.

"The result was I found myself surrounded. Towards dusk two trucks—they were packed full with fascists who didn't suspect a thing—came butting into Dubki. We let the Germans go by as calmly as you please, peppered them from the flanks with our machine-guns and when they started scrambling out of the cars—gave them a taste of our bayonets. The Germans don't like that. Some of them managed to get away. Their officer dived into the bulrushes. He sat there in the water, only the tip of his nose showing. We found very important documents in his despatch case.

"We got the engines of those German cars started, all twenty-five of us hopped in, with Petrov and myself in the leading car and Shmelkov at the wheel. The sky was covered with clouds, not a single star could be seen, there was no moon yet. We kept on behind the German lines, going parallel with the front. An hour went by, two hours—we didn't meet a soul. To the west of us was the glow of a fire, to the east—firing and big explosions. The fires and the booming of the guns enabled us to get our bearings.

"Ahead of us should be a familiar village. We pulled up. Petrov jumped out:

" 'Permit me to reconnoitre.'

"Well, I thought—this is where the man's come to life and clean forgotten about his girl. 'Go ahead.' He crammed his pockets with hand grenades and off he went. How quickly, lightly, nimbly he slipped away. About forty minutes later came a rustling in the bushes and there he was, standing near the chauffeur's cabin:

" 'There's a column of fascist cars in the village.'

"Well, I thought—that's mighty unpleasant. But—it was the only road we could take—to the right. and left of us lay swamps and there was no sense in our turning back. Shmelkov said reassuringly:

" 'Get in chaps, we'll slip through.'

"Our steel helmets could pass as German in the dark, it was impossible to make out our badges—the only thing liable to give us away was our bayonets, typical Russian bayonets. I ordered the men to hold their rifles on their knees.

"Shortly after we saw three blue lights—the German 'stop signal' at the head of a motor transport column. Shmelkov switched on the headlights to dim; we could see seven-ton trucks loaded with cases, a black swastika on a white disk painted on the radiators. On one side of the road were three officers; they were looking in our direction, flashing electric pocket lamps. Shmelkov switched on the headlights to full; the officers pulled wry faces, shaded their eyes with their hands, while we, as calmly as you please, drove past that motor transport column, turning our heads away so as not to expose the Red Stars on our helmets. We stepped on the gas, passed through a tiny village—a nice, snug little place with silent huts hidden amidst blossoming apple and cherry trees—in which it must have been wonderful to live. The village was empty, the inhabitants had fled.

"In an open car near the tiny wooden church sat a

German officer with a wizened face and flabby Adam's apple; he was studying a map by the light of a pocket lamp. I just managed to grasp Petrov's arm—he was on the point of leaning out of the cabin and letting fly with a hand grenade.

"That officer, apparently, must have smelt a rat. We had left the village behind us when a twenty HP motorcycle with a machine-gunner in the sidecar overtook us. This time Petrov let fly with his hand grenade, and he did it so beautifully that the machine-gunner went flying out of his sidecar in our direction for about six feet, just as though he were in a hurry to tell us something; the driver, together with the motorcycle, crashed headlong into the ditch.

"We sped on in the dark with lights out. The glow of a big fire on the horizon cast a lurid glare on the black underbrush ahead of us: here was a small river with a wooden bridge. We slowed down. We heard a gruff order in German. We sat silently—our rifles and hand grenades on the ready. Coming towards us were the dim figures of two sentries. One of them stopped, the other came right up to the chauffeur's cabin and looked in, his nose pressed against the window. We looked each other in the eye.... Suddenly he nodded to me, nodded to me and whispered in broken Russian:

"'Rus, bridge don't go, there fascists will shoot....

"For about five kilometres we cut across the meadow, along the river bank, listening to the croaking of the frogs. We got onto a road and again we saw blue lights, we heard the clanking of iron—tanks on the march, the leading tank being about thirty yards from us.

"'Lie flat,' I said to the men, 'and for heaven's sake keep your rear-ends out of sight.'

"We kept to the roadside. We drove on at a leisurely rate respectfully giving the right of way to the heavy black tanks with the swastika painted on a white disk looking for all the world like an eye. The fascists presume that the skull and crossbones of theirs, for example, on the tabs of their tunics, their black tanks and screaming bombs are enough to cause panicky fear to their enemies. Maybe ... they ought to know. Some savages don masks with fangs and horns when they are out on the warpath—also for the purpose of arousing terror....

"After those tanks came anti-aircraft guns, gasoline tank cars and trucks. It was as plain as pie—if we didn't look out we'd be in for it! We had to get onto another road. But how? Just try—we'd immediately arouse suspicion.

"To our right we caught sight of a birch alley. Shmelkov took the situation in at a glance and turned into it; whitewashed tree trunks flashed by and we drove right into the yard of a sovkhoz garage.

"Shmelkov swung the car around and began to back it as though intending to refuel. Several German soldiers came running up to open the doors of the garage. It's a good thing Hitler didn't teach them to use their brains and use them quickly. Shmelkov, our second car right behind us, swung round and, with the lights off, went racing down the birch-tree alley. Behind us we heard a yell and some shots but we were already on the road where that same column of cars was moving. We drove on like people who had every right to do so, who had just refuelled, sped past the tanks and turned off the road into a field of tall corn.

"At dawn we reached a small wood and here our supply of fuel gave out. We hid the trucks and sat down to have a bite. Suddenly, Petrov, a biscuit between his teeth, cocked his head, jumped to his feet and dived into the bracken—something had squeaked there—and back he came dragging a youngster of about nine by the arm, close-cropped, snub-nosed, with eyes flashing fire.

" 'Wharra you up to? Can't you see—I'm one of us. Lemme alone,' the youngster cried. 'I took you for fascists....'

" 'What are you doing here, young spitfire?'

" 'I'm a scout. I'm working with Grandpa Oksen. . . .'

"It turned out that this youngster, and five other young ragamuffins like him, had remained behind in the homestead together with eighty-year-old Grandpa Oksen. The men and women, taking their children and livestock with them, had made for the marshy woodlands and were doing a bit of guerilla fighting from there. Grandpa Oksen's homestead served as their headquarters. The six boys snooped about the district all day long, weren't afraid even to go right up to the Germans, snivelling as though they were begging for a crust, nosing around, prying into things, and in the evening they brought whatever information they had to the old man at the homestead. The partisans would make their way there at night and the old man assigned them their various jobs: in such-and-such a place the staff of some unit was quartered—it had to be wiped out, in another place a consignment of gasoline had been delivered, a tank unit had just arrived which had to be blown up.

"That boy was really bright. Before the sun was up he had led us to the other end of the woods—and did he crawl! The young devil wriggled just like a lizard through the grass, we could hardly manage to keep up with him. There, on the fringe of the woods, were fuelling tanks and five fighter planes.

"We settled that job in next to no time. When the shots fired by my snipers rang out and the German sentries who had been pacing up and down near their trenches in order to keep awake went sprawling onto the ground, we jumped out from behind the bushes: 'Hurrah!' This cheer of ours always has a bad effect on the Germans' nerves, a thing which can't be said about their screaming bombs on our men's nerves. The fascists came tumbling out from under the ground, from their dugouts —some of them put their hands up at once, others went rushing around—as if they were off their nuts, firing from their automatic rifles. We dragged one flier out of a fighter plane by his parachute straps. We set fire to the tank cars and planes and went back into the woods. The boy said to us:

" 'I'll be running along. So long. I'll tell Grandpa, he was planning to send a big group to this aerodrome....'

"We stayed where we were the whole day. We heard tanks going by. They combed the woods with their machine guns, but we were well under cover. We decided to make our way at night along the Dvina, on the lookout for a weak point. The fascists don't have a solid front— they advance headlong, in narrow wedges—and—well, with a bit of brains—one can always slip through.

"We set out at night, marching in deployed order, with machine-guns on the flanks. The town of 'D' was burning in the distance. It was one mass of flames, the columns of fire reached almost to the clouds. The fascists are fond of this kind of illumination, they prefer it to the movies. Aeroplanes circled over the burning city, firing on those who were trying to get away, driving the old folks, men, women and children, back into the flames.

"But enough of that.... We were furious—we were simply itching to get at them. We stopped a passenger car with three officers in it and, before popping them off, made them turn their ugly mugs in the direction of 'D' so that the sight of it would seem less amusing to them than the movies. We cut a heap of communication lines; attacked a motor transport column of twelve tank cars, wiped out the convoy, let the gasoline out and set fire to it. Golly, we weren't any too pleased after we'd done that: the illumination was too bright. We got onto the trail of three tanks which were crawling along at a leisurely pace and were real sorry we had no bottles with liquid fuel with us. Nevertheless, Petrov and two hand-grenade dischargers, collecting from the men quite a supply of hand grenades, dashed ahead, took cover on the roadside, and let fly with bundles of hand grenades —each at his own particular target. The leading tank reared, the other two were crippled—they could do nothing but fire at random into the darkness.

"And so we went on all night long, over fields and through woods, until we reached a homestead in which the Germans apparently had not been yet. We looked into one house, then into another, the shutters were up and—not a sign of life in the yards; suddenly, on one of the huts, on the thatched roof, a cock began to crow —heralding the dawn. Looking around we saw a stocky, bald-headed old man and a shrivelled old woman standing on the porch, awaiting death.

" 'Dad,' she says, 'they look like our men....'

"She began blessing us and kissing us in turn. But we—we were in no mood to go kissing with the old lady—we were as hungry as hunters. The old man brought out a loaf of bread, cut it up and handed us out thick slices which the old lady smeared with honey: 'Eat, duckies,' she repeated over and over again, 'eat....'

"To spend the day there was inconvenient. The old man got into his clothes, put on his sheepskin hat and led us through the marshy woods to a village where the partisan detachment had its hospital. The whole village came running out to greet us, the women invited us into their huts. We couldn't, after all, offend the good folks, we had to concede to their wishes: the wayfarer is lean and dusty, according to the good old custom he has to be washed and fed and taken care of. The women helped us get our things off, tended to our blisters— bathed them, gave us clean socks and treated us to everything they had in their ovens.

"Petrov—I noticed—was his old sentimental self again, the same old far-away, soft look in his eyes.... The peasants tried to talk us into staying behind, to join forces with their partisan unit.... And wouldn't we have liked to.... But after all—duty is duty...."

12

Lieutenant Zhabin sprang lightly to his feet.... "Enemy planes!" He snapped out an order. The tall grass in the hazel grove came to life. Five fascist bombers could be seen flying at a high altitude. In less than three minutes after the signaller's post had notified the aerodrome—a unit of our fighter planes appeared in the sky. Like taut strings they sang—threateningly, powerfully—as they climbed up steeply, heading for the bombers.... And the heavy fascist machines, dipping their wings, made to turn back. But it was too late.... The faint rat-tat-tat of machine-gun bursts could be heard from the pallid-blue sky. The fighter planes were hot on their tracks. One of the bombers reeled, then nose-dived towards the ground, leaving a trail of smoke after it....

MIKHAIL SHOLOKHOV

H a t e

"...YOU CANNOT DEFEAT AN ENEMY WITHOUT HAV-
ING LEARNT TO HATE HIM FROM THE BOTTOM
OF YOUR HEART."

*(From the May Day Order of the Day of the
People's Commissar of Defence, Comrade Stalin.)*

TREES, like people, each meet with their own destiny
in wartime. I have seen a huge tract of woodland
cut down by our artillery fire. Here, quite recently, the
Germans driven out of the village of "X" had entrenched
themselves and had thought to make a prolonged stay,
but death mowed them down with the trees. Under the
felled trunks of the pines lay German dead, their mangled
bodies rotting among the living green of fern and bracken;
and all the resinous fragrance of shell-splintered pine
was powerless to drown that stiflingly-sickly, pungent
stench of decaying bodies. Even the earth itself with its
dun-coloured scorched and brittle-edged shell-holes gave
off, it seemed, the odour of the grave....

Silently, majestically, death held sway in that clearing,
made and ploughed up by our shells; solitary, in the
very middle of it, stood a brave silver birch that had
survived by some miracle, and the breeze swayed its
splinter-scratched boughs and whispered in the young,
glazed and gluey leaves.

We were going through the clearing. The young
signaller just ahead of me touched the tree-trunk lightly,
asked with sincere and affectionate astonishment:

14

"How did you ever manage to come through it, my sweet?"

But if a pine that is hit by a shell perishes as though mowed with a scythe, leaving only the spinous crown oozing pine-tar, the oak tree meets its death otherwise.

A German shell landed in the trunk of an ancient oak growing on the bank of a nameless stream. The yawning, jagged wound sapped the life from half the tree, but the other half bowed by the explosion towards the water, revived marvellously in the springtime and burst into luxuriant leaf. And to this day, no doubt, the lower boughs of that mutilated oak bathe in running water while the upper still hold out eagerly to the sunlight their chiselled, reluctantly-unfolding leaves.

* * *

Tall, rather stooped, with something of the kite in his high, broad shoulders Lieutenant Gerassimov was sitting at the entrance of the dugout, giving us a circumstantial account of today's action, the enemy tank-attack repulsed by his battalion.

His lean face was calm, almost indifferent, his inflamed eyes screwed up wearily. He spoke in a cracked bass and from time to time interlaced his big knotty fingers: it was curiously out of keeping with his strong frame, his manly, vital countenance—his gesture so eloquent of wordless grief or profound and painful reverie.

Suddenly he ceased speaking and a change came over his face: the olive cheeks paled, the muscles twitched in the hollows beneath the cheekbones, and the eyes gazing steadily before him lit up with such a fierce and inextinguishable hatred that I involuntarily turned to follow the direction of his glance. Three German prisoners were passing through the wood from our nearest defence line and behind them came a Red Armyman in a summer tunic faded almost white by the sun, his trench cap on the back of his head.

15

The Red Armyman trudged on at a leisurely pace, the rifle in his hand swinging rhythmically to his movement, the knife-like bayonet flashing in the sunlight. And the Germans dawdled on too, dragging their feet shod in low boots splashed with yellow mud.

The foremost German—an elderly man with hollow cheeks overgrown with a bristly brown beard—cast a glowering, wolfish glance at the dugout as he passed, then turned sharply away and adjusted the helmet attached to his belt. Then Lieutenant Gerassimov sprang to his feet and barked at the Red Armyman:

"What are you up to? Taking'em for a stroll or what? Now then, get a move on and more sprightly."

He evidently wanted to add something else but lost his breath in his excitement. Turning sharply, he ran down the steps into the dugout. The political instructor who happened to be present, volunteered a reply to my inquiring, astonished glance.

"Can't be helped," he said in an undertone. "It's his nerves. He was taken prisoner by the Germans—didn't you know? You ought to talk to him sometime. Went through an awful lot there, and naturally he can't bear the sight of a live German after that—yes, particularly a live German. He doesn't mind looking at dead ones, I'd say he even got a certain satisfaction out of it, but let him only catch sight of prisoners and he either shuts his eyes and sits tight, all hot and cold, pale as death, or turns away and clears out."

The political instructor moved nearer and dropped his voice to a whisper. "I went into action with him twice. He's as strong as a horse, and you ought to see what he does.... I've seen a thing or two in my time, but the way he lays about him with butt and bayonet—I tell you, man, there's something terrifying about it!"

* * *

That night the German heavy artillery kept up a perturbing fire. At regular intervals there would be a dull rumble in the distance, followed a few seconds later by the metallic hiss of a shell high above in the starry sky; the drone would rise to a scream and gradually die away till somewhere at our backs, in the direction of the highway, crowded in the daytime with trucks bringing up munitions to the firing line, there would be a spurt of yellow lightning flame and an explosion like a thunder-clap.

In the pauses between the bursts, when silence fell on the woods once more, you could hear the thin whine of the gnats and the diffident croaking of startled frogs from the neighbouring swamp.

We were lying under a hazel bush and Lieutenant Gerassimov was leisurely giving us his story, beating off the gnats with a branch meanwhile. I give the story here as far as I can remember it.

"Before the war I was a mechanic in one of the mills in Western Siberia. I was called up last year—the ninth of July, to be exact. I've got a family, a wife and two children, and then there's my father, he's disabled. Well, my wife, naturally, cried a bit when she saw me off and sped me on my way with parting instructions: 'Defend your country and your folks to the last. Lay down your life if need be but we've got to win through!' I remember I laughed then and I said to her: 'Who do you think you are, my wife or the family agitator? I guess I'm big enough to know myself what I'm about and as for winning through—we'll wring it out of the fascists, by the throat, don't you worry.'

"My dad's made of tougher stuff, of course, but I didn't get off without a bit of parting advice from him either. 'Remember, Victor,' he said, 'that the name of the Gerassimovs is no ordinary name. You come of a line of workingmen; your great grandfather worked for Stroganov; our family's been turning out the country's iron for hundreds of years, and you've got to be like iron in this war. The government we have is of our own making, it made you a commander of the reserves even before the war broke out and you've got to let the enemy have it good and hard.'

" 'We will, dad,' I said.

"On the way to the station I dropped in at the District Party Committee headquarters. Our secretary was a dry, matter-of-fact chap given to reasoning and I thought to myself—well, if my wife and my old man simply couldn't desist from giving me some parting advice this fellow will surely never let me go without a rigmarole that'll last half-an-hour at least. It turned out just the very opposite. 'Sit down, Gerassimov,' he says, 'it used to be the custom in the old days to sit down for a minute or two before taking a journey.'

"We sat still for a bit, and then he stood up and I saw that his spectacles looked sort of blurred.... Well, I thought to myself, wonders are happening today. And then he said: 'There's nothing much to be said, Comrade Gerassimov. I remember you when you were just so high, a lop-eared youngster wearing a Pioneer's red kerchief. And I remember you afterwards as a League member, and I've known you as a member of the Party for ten years now. Show no mercy to those German swine! The Party organization has confidence in you.' For the first time in my life we kissed each other in the old Russian custom—and somehow that secretary didn't seem such a dry old stick as he used to.

"And I felt so warmed by the affectionate way he treated me that I came out of the District Committee building gladdened and moved.

"My wife, too, put me in a more cheerful frame of mind. You can well understand it's not a particularly cheerful business for any man's wife—having to see her husband off to the front. Well, and mine also got a bit upset, she wanted to say something really important but everything had gone clean out of her head. The train

18

was just pulling out and she ran alongside, wouldn't let go of my hand and kept on repeating:

" 'See you look after yourself, Vitya, and don't catch cold out there at the front.' 'Good heavens, Nadia,' I said, 'what do you take me for? I shouldn't think of catching cold. It's a very healthy and even temperate climate out there.' And I felt at the same time sad at parting from her and cheered up by the silly but sweet things she said. And then a quiet anger at the Germans took hold of me. Since you were the first to start, my fine treacherous neighbours—you'd better look out. We'll give you the drubbing of your life."

He was silent for a few minutes, listening to the spasmodic exchange of machine-gun fire on the forward fringe. It ceased as unexpectedly as it had begun.

"Before the war we used to get machinery from Germany. When I was assembling it, I remember, I used to examine every part five or six times, turning it over and looking at it from every side. There was no doubt about it, skilful hands had made those machines. I used to read books by German writers and somehow I'd got into the way of respecting the German people. True, I used to think at times what a shame it was that a people so gifted and industrious should stand that abominable Hitlerite regime. . . . But that, after all, was their own affair. . . . Then the war broke out in Western Europe. . . .

"And so I was on my way to the front and I couldn't help thinking: their army's a pretty good one and they are very strong on the technical side. Why, when you come to think of it, it's really interesting to cross swords with an enemy like that and break his ribs. We weren't so simple either, in 1941. I must admit I never looked for any very honest scruples in this adversary of ours— you can't expect anything of that sort when you're dealing with fascism—but still I never thought I'd have to fight such a downright unprincipled gang as the Germans actually turned out to be. But, we'll come to that later on. . . .

"Our unit reached the front at the end of July. Early on the morning of the twenty-seventh we went into action. At first, being new to it—it was a bit terrifying. They gave us hell with their trench mortars but towards evening we'd got the hang of things, knocked them about a bit, and dislodged them from one of the villages. We rounded up a bunch of them, about fifteen in all, in that engagement. I remember it clearly as if it had only just happened. They were brought in looking frightened and pale. My men had cooled down already by then and each brought the prisoners what he could spare: a bit of tobacco or a fag, some gave them tea. And they clapped them on the back and called them 'camarade.' 'What are you fighting for, camarade,' and all that sort of thing.

"One of our fellows, a man with many years' service to his record, watched this touching scene a while and then he said: 'Chuck slobbering over these friends of yours. Here they're all 'camarades.' 'Wait till you see what they're doing behind their own lines, how they treat our wounded men and civilians.' Well, his words had about the same effect as if he'd poured a bucket of cold water over us. And then he walked off.

"Soon after that our troops launched an offensive and then we actually did see what they were doing . . . villages razed to the ground, hundreds of women, children and old folks shot, mutilated corpses of Red Army prisoners, women and girls, some only children, raped and then most brutally done to death.

"One case in particular sticks in my mind: it was a girl of about eleven. She must have been on her way to school when the Germans caught her, dragged her into a garden, raped and then killed her. There she lay among the crushed potato tops, a chit of a girl, a mere child, with her schoolbooks lying all around bespattered with her blood. . . . Her face was frightful, gashed with

20

sabre cuts. She was still clutching her school-satchel and it was open. We covered the body with a cape and stood a minute or two by it in silence. Then the men went away just as silently. But I lingered on, whispering over and over, I remember in a sort of daze: 'Barkov and Polovinkin. Physical geography reader for higher-grade schools.' It was the title of one of the books lying there in the grass. A book I knew. Because my own little girl was in the fifth form. . . .

"This was near Ruzhin. At Skviri, the place of execution was in a gully. This was where the captured Red Armymen had been tortured to death. You've most likely been in a butcher shop, haven't you? Well, that'll give you an idea of what this place looked like. . . .

"The trunks of the bodies clotted with blood hung from the boughs of the trees growing in the gully. The hands and feet had been hacked off; and half the skin was flayed off. . . . The bodies of eight more men lay in a heap at the bottom of the gully. And you couldn't tell to which man the limbs belonged. It was just a pile of slaughtered flesh hacked into big pieces. And stacked on top of them, like plates, one fitting into the other, were eight Red Army trench caps. . . .

"You think perhaps, that it's possible to convey in words all that I've seen. No! It's impossible. There are no words to describe it. You have to see it yourself. And anyhow it's about time we changed the subject," and Lieutenant Gerassimov said nothing for a long time.

"Can one smoke here?" I asked.

"Yes, of course, but don't show a light," he replied in a hoarse voice and having lit up himself, he went on:

"You can understand that after seeing all that the Germans have done we've become pretty furious ourselves. It's only to be expected. Everyone of us realized that we weren't dealing with human beings but with foul beasts, drunk with blood. It was apparent that the Germans kill, rape and murder our people with the same thoroughness they once applied to making lathes and machinery. Then we had to fall back again, but we kept on fighting like devils, though, all the time.

"Nearly all the men in my company were Siberians. But we put up a stubborn fight for every inch of Ukrainian soil. Many a man from my parts was killed in the Ukraine, but the Germans had to pay a heavier price still. Yes, we were losing ground but we let them have it hot just the same."

He took a pull or two at his cigarette, then he went on in a different modulated tone of voice.

"Fine soil in the Ukraine, and the surroundings are lovely too. Every village, every hamlet, seemed near and dear to us. Maybe it's because we hadn't stinted our blood to defend them, and blood, they say, is thicker than water.... And when we had to withdraw from one of those villages our hearts ached, ached like the very dickens. You felt sorry, so devilishly sorry. Here we were abandoning a place for the time being, and we simply could not look each other in the eyes.

"... Little did I think at the time that I'd ever be a prisoner of the Germans. But that's what happened. I was wounded in September for the first time, but I stayed on with my company. And on the twenty-first I was wounded for the second time in the fighting around Denisovka, Poltava Region, and taken prisoner.

"The German tanks had broken through on our left flank and their infantry came pouring through the breach right on their heels. We were surrounded but we fought our way through. That day my company suffered particularly heavy losses. We repulsed two tank attacks, set fire to or crippled six of the enemy's tanks and an armoured car and accounted for some hundred and twenty Hitlerites in a maize-field. But at this point they brought up their trench-mortar batteries and we were obliged to abandon the elevation which we'd held from midday till four o'clock. The weather had been sultry since morning. Not a cloud in the sky and the sun blazing down till you felt you couldn't breathe. Shells were coming over thick and fast and I remember, we were so thirsty that the men's lips were swollen black and I was issuing orders in a hoarse croak that I didn't recognize as my own voice. We were crossing a glade when a shell burst right in front of me. I saw, I remember vaguely, a pillar of black earth and dust and—that's all. A shell splinter went through my helmet, a second got me in the right shoulder.

"I don't remember how long I lay there unconscious, but the tramping of feet brought me to myself. Raising my head, I saw that I wasn't lying in the place where I had fallen. My tunic was gone and my shoulder had been roughly bandaged. I had lost my helmet, too. There was a bandage round my head but it hadn't been properly fastened and the end trailed down on my chest. It flashed through my mind that my men must have carried me off the field and bandaged me on the way and it was them I hoped to see when after much difficulty I raised my head. But running towards me were not my men— but Germans! It was the tramp of their feet that had brought me back to consciousness. I could see them perfectly clear now, just as though on a cinema screen. I groped about me: neither revolver nor rifle nor even a hand grenade were within reach. Someone—one of my own men probably—had relieved me of my arms and despatch case.

"'So this is the end,' I thought to myself. Of what else was I thinking at that moment? If what you have in mind is material for a future novel, you'd better fill in the gaps yourself. To tell the truth, I hadn't time to think of anything just then. The Germans were close at hand and I didn't want to die lying down. I simply didn't want to. I just couldn't meet the end lying down, you understand? So I made a terrific effort and got up

23

on my knees, touching the ground with my hands to steady myself.

"By the time they reached me I was on my feet. Yes, I stood there, rather groggy, and terribly afraid that any moment my knees would give way and they'd finish me off with their boyonets while I'd be down. I can't recall a single face now. They clustered around me talking and laughing. 'Kill me, you blackguards!' I said. 'Kill me and be done with it, before I fall.' One of them hit me with his rifle—but I managed to get up again. They burst out laughing and one of them waved his hand as much as to say: get a move on. I did.

"My face was caked with blood from the wound in my head, and blood was still streaming from it all warm and sticky, my shoulder ached, and I couldn't raise my right hand. I remember now that all I wanted was to lie down and not go anywhere, but still—I went on....

"No, I certainly didn't want to die, and even less did I want to stay a prisoner. With a tremendous effort, fighting down my dizziness and sickness, I plodded on; so there was life in me yet, and I could still act. But oh, how the thirst tormented me! My mouth was parched and all the time though my feet went on of themselves, a sort of black mist seemed to be billowing before my eyes. I was on the verge of unconsciousness but I went on, thinking to myself: 'As soon as I get a drink and a bit of a rest, I'll make a dash for it!'

"All of us who had been taken prisoner were assembled on the fringe of the woods and lined up. They were men from a neighbouring unit of ours. From my own regiment I recognized only two Red Armymen—from the 3rd Company. Most of the prisoners were wounded.

"A German lieutenant demanded to know, in broken Russian, if there were any commissars and commanders among us. Nobody answered. Then he snapped out: 'Commissars and officers—two paces forward march!' Nobody budged.

"The lieutenant paced slowly in front of the line and picked out about fifteen or sixteen men who looked more or less like Jews. He asked each of them 'Jude?' and, without waiting for an answer, ordered the man to fall out. The men he picked out included not only Jews but Armenians and Russians who happened to be swarthy and have black hair. They were led off a little distance away and shot down before our eyes by a burst from automatics. Then we were submitted to a rather perfunctory search, and deprived of our pocket books and other personal belongings. I was never in the habit of carrying my Party card in my pocket book: it was in an inside pocket of my pants, that's why they overlooked it. Men are queer creatures, when you come to think of it: I knew for certain that my life hung on a thread, that even if I wasn't killed when I attempted to escape, I'd be sure to be killed on the road because I'd lost so much blood and I wouldn't be able to keep up with the rest. And yet when the search was over and I knew I still had my Party card on me, I was so glad, that I actually forgot all about my thirst.

"We were lined up and driven off westward. A pretty strong convoy kept the roadsides, and in addition a dozen German motorcyclists brought up the rear. We were kept going at a quick pace and my strength was ebbing fast. I fell twice, but each time I scrambled to my feet and went on because I knew that if I stayed down a minute longer than was necessary the column would pass on, and I would be shot then and there in the roadway. That was what happened to a sergeant just ahead of me. He'd been wounded in the leg and could hardly drag himself along. He groaned terribly and sometimes even shrieked with pain. We'd gone about a kilometre when he cried out:

" 'No, I can't stick it any longer. Goodbye, comrades!' and sat down in the middle of the road.

"The others tried to give him a hand but he slumped

down again on the ground. I remember him like someone in a dream—the drawn, pale, youthful face, the knitted brows, and eyes wet with tears of pain. The column passed on. He was left behind. I glanced round, and I saw a man on a motorcycle ride up close to him and, without getting off his bike, pull out his pistol, shove it against the sergeant's ear and fire. Before we reached the river the Germans shot several more of the Red Armymen who fell behind.

"And now we came in sight of the river, the ruined bridge and a truck that'd got stuck at the side of the crossing. And right there I fell face downwards. Did I faint? No, I didn't. I just measured my length in the road and my mouth was full of dust. I ground my teeth in fury, I could feel the sand gritty between my teeth, but I couldn't get up. My comrades were marching past me. 'Get up quick!' one of them said in a low voice as he passed, 'or they'll do you in.' I started to tear my mouth with my fingers, press hard on my eyeballs so that the pain would rouse me and help me to get to my feet again. . . .

"The column had passed on and my ear caught the swish of the motor-bike wheels coming towards me. Somehow I did manage to struggle to my feet! Without glancing at the motorcyclist, and staggering like a drunken man, I forced myself to overtake the column and fell into line somewhere at the back. Crossing the river, the tanks and trucks stirred up the mud in the water, but we drank of it gratefully—that warm, brown slush, and it seemed sweeter to us than the purest spring water. I splashed my head and shoulder with it. That refreshed me and my strength came back to me. Now I could trudge on in the hope that I would not drop and be left lying in the roadway. . . .

"Hardly had we left the river behind us when we met a column of German medium tanks. The driver of the leading tank, seeing that we were prisoners, stepped on the gas and drove full tilt into our column. The front ranks were mangled and crushed under the treads. The motorcyclists and the rest of the convoy roared laughing at the sight, bawled something to the tank crews, who had popped their heads out of the hatches, and waved their hands. Then they lined us up again and drove us along by the side of the road. Oh yes, they've a queer sense of humour—the Germans, there's no doubt about it....

"That evening and night I made no attempt to escape, as I realized that I wouldn't be able to do it—I was too weak from loss of blood. Besides, a strict watch was kept over us, and any attempt at escape would be bound to have ended badly. But how I cursed myself afterwards for not having made the attempt! Next morning we were driven through a village where a German unit was stationed. The German infantrymen trooped out into the road to look at us, and the convoy made us go through that village at the double. They wanted to humiliate us before the German soldiers who were just coming up to the front. And we did it at the double. Whoever lagged behind or fell, was shot at once. By evening we had reached the war prisoners' camp.

"This actually was the yard of some machine-and-tractor station well fenced off with barbed wire. Prisoners were huddled inside, shoulder to shoulder. We were handed over to the camp guard and they drove us inside with blows of rifle-butts. To call that camp hell would be calling it nothing at all. For one thing, there was no latrine. Men had to relieve themselves where they stood and then sit or lie in filth and stinking pools. The weaker of us never got up at all. We were given food and water once a day—that is to say, we got a mug of water and a handful of raw millet or mildewed sunflower seed. Nothing else. Some days they forgot to give us anything at all....

"After a day or two heavy rains set in. The slush

and mud was up to our knees by now. Of mornings the men, drenched to the skin steamed like horses; and the rain never ceased.... Several dozen of the prisoners died every night. We were getting weaker and weaker for want of food. And my wounds troubled me a lot.

"By the sixth day I felt that my head and shoulder were much worse. The wounds were suppurating. Then they started to smell. Alongside the camp there were collective farm stables, where seriously wounded Red Armymen were lying. In the morning I went to the sergeant of the guard and asked leave to see the doctor who, as I had been told, was with the wounded. The German NCO spoke Russian quite well. 'Go to your doctor, Russian,' he replied. 'He's sure to help you right away.'

"I didn't understand the sneer then, and, pleased to have got leave, made the best of my way to the stables.

"The army doctor met me at the door. He was a finished man, I could see at once. Thin to the point of emaciation, worn out, he was already half out of his mind with all he had gone through. The wounded lay about on manure litter, suffocating with the abominable stench. The wounds of most of them were crawling with maggots and those of the wounded who were able to do so, dug out these maggots with their finger nails and sticks.... Beside them lay a pile of dead prisoners that no one had time to clear away.

"'See that?' the doctor said. 'So how can I help you? I haven't a bandage or anything. Clear out, for God's sake. Take those dirty bandages off and sprinkle ashes on the wounds. There's some fresh ashes at the door.'

"I did as he advised. The German NCO met me at the door. He was smiling broadly. 'Well, how did you get on? Oh, your soldiers have a splendid doctor. Did he give you any help?' I wanted to pass him without speaking but he punched me in the face and shouted: 'So you won't answer me, you swine!' I fell, and he started kicking me in the chest and head, and he went at it until he was dead tired. I'll never forget that German as long as I live, never. He beat me up several times after that. As soon as he'd catch sight of me through the barbed wire, he'd order me out and start to beat me in a silent, concentrated sort of way....

"You wonder how I stood it all? Before the war, and before I became a mechanic, I worked as longshoreman on the River Kama, and I could carry two sacks of salt, each a hundredweight, at one time. Yes, I was pretty strong, nothing to complain of, and in general I have a sound constitution. But the chief thing here was—I didn't want to die, my will to resistance was so strong. I had to get back to the army, among the men who were fighting for their country—and I did get back eventually, to avenge myself on my enemies to the very end!

"From that camp, which appeared to be a distributing centre, I was transferred to another about a hundred kilometres away. It didn't differ at all from the first one: the same tall posts with barbed wire around them, and not a bit of roofing over the prisoners' heads—nothing. And the food was just the same, except that, occasionally, we got a mug of mouldy grain that was supposed to have been cooked instead of the raw millet, or they would drag in the carcasses of some dead horses and let the prisoners divide the meat up among themselves. We ate it so as not to die of starvation and hundreds of our men died of it.... Then, to make matters worse, the cold weather set in; in October it rained without ever stopping, and there were frosts in the mornings. We suffered cruelly from cold. I managed to get a tunic and a coat off one of the prisoners who died, but even these didn't protect me from the cold. We were used to hunger by then.

"The soldiers who guarded us were well-fed—fattened on what they were stealing. They were all tarred with the same brush. A choicer selection of scoundrels would

29

be hard to find. Their idea of entertainment ran on the following lines. In the morning a corporal would come up to the barbed wire and announce through the interpreter: 'Rations will be given out just now. They'll be served out from the left side.'

"The corporal would leave. Every man able to stand on his feet would line up on the left side. And then we'd wait—an hour, two hours, even three hours. Hundreds of shivering, living skeletons standing in the piercing wind. Standing, waiting.

"Suddenly Germans would appear from the opposite side. They'd throw pieces of horse flesh over the wire entanglements. The whole crowd, craving with hunger, would stampede across. There would be a regular scrimmage over the bits of horsemeat smeared with mud.

"The Germans would roar. Then there'd be a prolonged burst of machine-gunning, shrieks and groans followed. The prisoners would run pell-mell to the left side again leaving the killed and wounded on the ground.... The lanky First Lieutenant—who was the superintendent of the camp—would then approach the barbed wire entanglement acompanied by the interpreter. Scarcely able to control his laughter, he would say:

"'It's been reported to me that a disgraceful scene took place during the distribution of rations. Should this occur again I'll have all of you Russian swine shot down without mercy. Clear away the killed and wounded!' The crowd of German soldiers behind the officer would be splitting their sides laughing. This was the sort of 'wit' they were fond of.

"In silence we dragged the dead away from the camp yard and buried them in the gully a little way off....

"In that camp we were beaten up regularly; they laid about us with their fists, sticks and butts. Sometimes they beat us out of sheer boredom, sometimes for amusement. My wounds were beginning to heal, then they opened again, either from the constant dampness or the beating, and the pain was almost unbearable. But I stood it, I lived through it all, still clinging to my hope of delivery.... We slept on the muddy ground, they wouldn't give us even a bit of straw. We would huddle close together and lie around like that. And all night the fidgeting would go on: those who were at the very bottom, in the mud, would freeze and those who were on top would be just as cold. There was neither sleep nor rest, but only bitter torment.

"So the days went by as in an evil dream and with every day I grew weaker. A child could have knocked me down. Sometimes I looked with horror at my skinny withered arms and wondered: 'How shall I ever get out of here?' And how I cursed myself for not having attempted to escape the first days. If they'd have killed me, I would have been spared all this ghastly torture.

"Winter came. We cleared away the snowdrifts and slept on the frozen ground. Our numbers were dwindling steadily.... At last it was announced that in a few days' time we were to be sent to work. We all brightened up. Hope stirred in everybody's breast, faint enough, but still a hope that somehow we might get a chance to escape.

"That night it was very still and frosty. Just before daybreak we heard the booming of artillery. The people around me awoke to life. And when the rumble of guns came again someone cried out:

"'Comrades, it's our troops—attacking!'

"What followed is well-nigh inconceivable. The whole camp was on its feet, even those who hadn't been able to get up for days. All around you could hear feverish whispering and stifled sobbing.... Someone near me was crying, just like a woman does.... And me too.... Me too...."

Lieutenant Gerassimov's voice broke as he said this quickly. After a short pause, he pulled himself together and went on in a quieter tone: "The tears rolled down my cheeks, too, and froze in the chill wind.... Someone started to sing the 'Internationale' in a feeble voice: It was taken up by our cracked piping voices. The sentries opened fire on us with rifles and automatics. An order was snapped out: 'Lie down!' I lay flat, pressing my body close to the snow; and cried like a child. Yes, but they were tears of pride as well as joy, pride in our people. The Germans could kill us, unarmed and enfeebled as we were with hunger, could torture us, but they hadn't been able to break our spirit and never would! They've got hold of the wrong kind for that, I'm telling you straight."

* * *

I didn't hear the end of Lieutenant Gerassimov's story that night. He received an urgent summons from headquarters. We met again a few days later. The dugout smelled of mildew and pine-tar. He was sitting on a bench, leaning forward, the huge bony wrists resting on his knees, the fingers interlocked. As I looked at him, it occurred to me that probably in the prison-camp he had got into the habit of sitting for hours like that, with his fingers interlocked, sitting silent, lost in gloomy, oppressive, fruitless meditation....

"You want to know how I managed to escape? This is how it happened. Soon after that night when we'd heard the rumbling of guns, we were put to work building fortifications. The frosts had been followed by a thaw. It was raining. We were marched off in a northerly direction from the camp. On the road we had a repetition of what had been before: people dropped with exhaustion, they were shot and left there....

"One of the men, by the way, was shot by a German NCO for picking up a frozen potato. We were crossing a potato-plot. The man in question, a sergeant, a Ukrainian, by name of Gonchar, picked up the blasted potato and wanted to hide it. The NCO saw him. Without saying a word he went up to Gonchar and shot him through the back of the head. The column was ordered to halt and line up again. 'All this is German property!' the NCO explained, indicating everything with a sweep of his arm. 'Any one of you who touches anything without permission, will be shot.'

"On the way we had to pass through a village. The women, directly they saw us, came out and threw us pieces of bread and baked potatoes. Some of us managed to pick them up, others didn't: the convoy opened fire on the windows of the houses and we were ordered to quicken our step. But the children—there's no frightening them! They ran out into the roadway a good way ahead of us, and left the bread there, so as we could pick it up without delay as we went along. I got a great big boiled potato, I remember. I shared it with the man next to me. We ate it, skin and all, and I'm sure I've never tasted anything so delicious in my life!

"The fortifications we were put to work on were in the woods. The guard was strengthened and we were given spades. But it wasn't of building for them that I was thinking; I wanted to destroy.

"The evening of that same day I made up my mind: I scrambled out of the pit we were digging, took up my spade in my left hand, and went up to the guard.... I had noticed that the rest of the Germans were some distance away, near a gully, and except for the man who was keeping watch over our group there wasn't another guard anywhere in sight.

"'Look, my spade's broken,' I muttered, going up to the soldier. For an instant it crossed my mind that if I couldn't muster enough strength to knock him down at the first blow, I was done for. The German must have noticed something in my face for he made a movement of his shoulder to unsling his automatic. Then I hit out with the spade, and caught him full in the face. I couldn't get at his head because he was wearing a helmet. Still, I had enough strength left to hit him hard and he dropped on his back without a sound....

"Now I had an automatic and three clips. I started to run. But I found that I couldn't. I hadn't the strength and that was all there was to it. I stopped, got my breath and started off again at a slow trot. The wood on the other side of the gully was thicker so I made for that. I can't recollect now how many times I fell, got up, fell again.... But I was getting farther away every minute. Half-sobbing, breathless with weariness, I had made my way at last to the grove on the other side of the hill, when far behind me came the rattle of a machine-gun and shouting. It wouldn't be so easy to catch me now.

"Dusk would be falling soon. But if the Germans did contrive to come upon my tracks and get near me—well, I would keep my last cartridge for myself. That thought sustained me, and I went on at an easier pace and more cautiously.

"That night I spent in the woods. There was a village about half-a-kilometre away but I was afraid to go near it, for fear of bumping into the Germans again.

"Next day I was picked up by some partisans. I stayed in their dugout for a couple of weeks till I got strong. At first they were rather suspicious of me, in spite of the fact that I showed them my Party card. I'd managed to sew it in the lining of my coat in camp. But afterwards, when I took part in their operations, their attitude to me underwent a change. It was there that I opened my account for the Germans I'd killed. and I keep the account very carefully till now; the figures are mounting gradually, nearing the hundred mark.

"In January the partisans smuggled me across the lines. I was about a month in the hospital. They got the splinter out of my shoulder there, and as for the rest of my ailments, the rheumatism I'd got in the camp and so on, well, that will just have to wait until the war is over. Then I was sent home from the hospital to recuperate. I was a week at home. I couldn't stand it any more. I just got a yearning to be back; after all my place is here, to the very end."

* * *

At the entrance to the dugout we said goodbye. Gazing out thoughtfully over the sunlit forest clearing Lieutenant Gerassimov said:

"...And we've learnt to fight the real proper way, and hate and love. War is the whetstone that grinds all feelings fine. You'd think that love and hate couldn't be placed side by side. You know the old saying: 'The stallion and the timid hind—never in one harness bind.' And here you can see them harnessed and pulling well together! Bitter hatred is what I feel for the Germans, for all they've done to my country and to me, and at the same time I love my people with all my heart and I want them never to suffer under the German yoke. That's what makes me, and all of us for that matter, fight so savagely; it's just these two feelings, embodied in action that will lead us to victory. And if love for our country is cherished in our hearts, and will be cherished untill those hearts cease to beat, still we always carry our hatred on the points of our bayonets. Forgive me if it's rather an elaborate way of expressing it, but that is what I think," concluded Lieutenant Gerassimov, and for the first time in our acquaintance he smiled—the candid smile of a child.

And now for the first time I noticed that this lieutenant of thirty-two, whose grim face bore traces of the harrowing experience he had been through, but still sturdy as an oak, had dazzlingly silvery white hair at the temples. And so pure was that hoary whiteness, won through great suffering, that the white thread of the spider's web clinging to his trench cap was lost against the gleaming white temple where I could not distinguish it, try as I might.

VALENTINE KATAYEV

The Flag*

THE SLATE covered roofs of a few houses could be seen in the centre of the island. Above them towered the narrow, triangled church with a straight black cross standing out in strong relief against the grey sky.

The rugged shore seemed to be devoid of life. For a hundred miles around, the sea, too, appeared a barren waste. But that was not so.

At times the faint outline of a naval vessel or transport would loom on the horizon far out at sea. And instantly, one of the granite boulders would move aside, noiselessly, lightly—as though in a dream or fairy tale—exposing a cave from the maw of which three long-range guns would rise smoothly to the surface, above the sea level, and then, gliding forward into place, come to a stop. Three muzzles of a fantastic length automatically followed the movements of the enemy vessel as though drawn by a magnet. The thick steel sections and the concentric grooves glistened with heavy, green oil.

The casemates, hewn far into the cliff, housed the small garrison of the fort, its supplies and equipment. A narrow recess, separated from the general mess by a plywood partition, served the commandant of the fort and the commissar as living quarters. They were sitting on

---

* This story is based on an actual occurrence.—*V. K.*

their bunks which fitted into the wall. Between them stood a small table on which burned an electric lamp. The disc of the ventilator reflected its rays in flashes like lightning. A dry wind rustled the stock sheets, sent a pencil rolling on the chart marked off in squares. It was a chart of the sea. The commandant had just received a report that an enemy destroyer had been sighted in square number eight. The commandant nodded his head.

A dazzling sheet of orange flame spurted from the guns. Three salvos in quick succession shook the water and the rocks, rending the air with a thunder that was almost deafening. With a clattering like that of iron balls sent rolling over marble, the shells sped on their way, one after the other. The returning echo, carried back over the water several minutes later, told that they had burst.

The commandant and the commissar looked at one another in silence. Everything was clear without any further words: the island was surrounded, communications cut; for over a month the handful of brave men had been defending the beleaguered fort against incessant attacks from sea and air; bombs rained down on the cliffs with furious persistency; torpedo boats and invasion boats nosed all around; the enemy was determined to take the island by storm; but the granite cliffs remained impregnable; the enemy had been forced to retire far out to sea; summoning his forces, re-arranging his lines, the enemy launched attack after attack, searching for some weak spot but never finding one.

Time passed.

The supply of munitions and food dwindled. The vaults grew empty. For hours at a stretch the commandant and the commissar pored over the stock sheets. They manœuvred, cut down supplies. They did their utmost to stave off the fateful hour. But the end drew ever nearer. Now it had come.

"Well?" the commissar asked finally.

"That's all," the commandant said. "The last."

"In that case—write."

The commandant, taking his time, opened the log book, glanced at the clock and wrote in his neat hand:

> "Today all guns have been in action since early morning. At 5.45 p.m. we fired our last salvo. Our supply of shells has run out. Supply of food—one day's ration."

He closed the log book—a heavy ledger, corded and sealed, held it for a while in his hand as though trying to determine its weight, and then put it back on the shelf.

"So there we are, commissar," he said gravely.

There was a knock on the door.

"Come in."

The officer on duty, his oilskins glistening from the raindrops which trickled down it, entered the room. He placed a small aluminium cylinder on the table.

"A pendant?"

"Yes, Comrade Commandant."

"How was it dropped?"

"By a German fighter plane."

The commandant unscrewed the lid, inserted two fingers into the cylinder and drew out a small roll of paper. He read it and a frown clouded his face. On the sheet of parchment, in a bold, legible hand, was written the following in blue alizarin ink:

> "Mister Commandant of the Soviet fort and batteries. You surrounded from every side are. Supplies of munitions and provisions no more you have. In order to avoiding the useless bloodshed I propose that you to capitulation agree. Conditions: All garrison of fort, together with Commandant and officers, must leave the batteries of fort intact and in good order and with no arms go to square near church—and there to surrender. At 6 a.m. Middle European time

a white flag on the church hoisted must be. For this I give you promise your lives to spare. No agree —death. Surrender.

Rear Admiral von Everscharp
Commander of the German Invasion Flotilla"

The commandant handed the conditions of capitulation to the commissar. The commissar read them through and said to the officer on duty:

"Very well, you can go."

The officer on duty left the room.

"So they want to see a flag on the church," the commandant said thoughtfully when they were alone again.

"Yes," the commissar said.

"They'll see it," the commandant said, getting into his greatcoat. "A big flag on the church. What do you think, commissar, will they notice it? We must see to it that they really do. It must be the biggest thing we can make. Will we have time?"

"We've time enough," the commissar replied, looking for his hat. "We have a whole night in which to get it done. We won't keep them waiting. We'll manage it in good time. The lads will do the job. It'll be something enormous. I give you my word for it."

The two men—commandant and commissar—embraced and kissed each other, right on the lips. It was a hearty embrace, a man's embrace, leaving on their lips the coarse taste of weather-beaten, bitter skin. They kissed each other for the first time in their lives, in accordance with the old Russian custom. They were in a hurry. They knew that they would have no further opportunity to say goodbye to each other.

The commissar went into the messroom, lifted the bust of Lenin from its pedestal and took away the red plush cloth on which it had been standing. After that he got onto a stool and took down the red bunting from the walls with the slogans inscribed upon it.

All night long the garrison of the fort was busy at work sewing a flag, an enormous flag, larger even than the floor of the messroom. It was sewn with big sailor's needles and coarse sailor's thread, from odd bits of material—everything suitable that the men had found in their chests.

Shortly before dawn the flag was ready.

The sailors then made themselves spick and span for the last time, donned new tunics and, one after the other, with their automatic rifles slung around their necks and their pockets crammed full of munitions, they filed out up the ladder to the surface.

* * *

At daybreak the orderly officer knocked at von Everscharp's cabin. Von Everscharp was not sleeping. He lay fully dressed on his bunk. He went up to his dressing table, glanced at himself in the mirror and wiped the pouches under his eyes with Eau de Cologne. Only after this did he give the orderly officer permission to enter the cabin. The orderly officer was in a state of great excitement. With an effort he mastered his feelings and raised his hand in salute.

"Is there a flag on the church?" von Everscharp asked dryly, fondling the twisted ivory hilt of his dirk.

"Yes sir. They're surrendering."

"Good," von Everscharp said. "You have brought me splendid news. Excellent. Call all hands on deck."

A minute later he was standing on the bridge, his legs wide apart. Dawn was just breaking, a bleak, windy, autumn dawn. Through his glasses von Everscharp could see the small granite island on the horizon. It lay in the midst of a grey, forbidding sea. Rugged waves in savage monotony repeated the lines of the jagged coast. The sea looked as though it was hewn out of granite.

Against the background of the fishing village towered the narrow, triangled church with a straight black cross standing out in strong relief against the murky sky. An enormous flag fluttered from the spire. In the murky light of the early dawn it stood out dark, almost black.

"Poor chaps," von Everscharp said, "they probably had to part with their last sheets in order to sew such an enormous white flag. Well, nothing can be done. Capitulations have their inconveniences."

He snapped out an order.

The flotilla of invasion boats and torpedo boats sped towards the island. The island grew in size, drew nearer. It was possible now, without the help of glasses, to see the handful of sailors standing on the square near the church.

Just then the sun peered out, a red flaming ball. It hung suspended in the air between the sky and the water, the upper rim hidden in a hazy cloud bank, the lower resting on the jagged surface of the sea. The island seemed enveloped in gloom. The flag on the church turned red, the colour of molten iron.

"Damn it all, its a beautiful sight," von Everscharp said, "the sun has dyed the white flag red. But we'll make it go white again shortly."

The wind lashed the waves into a heavy swell. They beat against the cliffs. Resisting the blows the cliffs rang like bronze. A silvery chime trembled in the spray moistened air. The waves rolled on, tinkled, whispered, then, suddenly, striking full blast against an unseen barrier, they would be sent hurtling back with the roar of a cannon shot, a veritable geyser of boiling, rosy-coloured spray.

The invasion boats reached the shore. Up to their chests in the foamy water, their automatic rifles held above their heads, the Germans leapt from boulder to boulder, slipping, falling, scrambling to their feet again, in a dash towards the fort. Now they had reached the cliff. Now they were making their way down the open hatch leading to the battery.

Von Everscharp stood where he was, his hands clutching the rails of the bridge. He could not tear his eyes away from the shore. The sight of the island being stormed held him enraptured. His face twitched convulsively.

"Forward, my lads, forward!"

Suddenly, an underground explosion of a gigantic force shook the island. Bloody shreds of clothes and human bodies went flying out of the hatch. The cliffs reeled against each other, splitting in two. They were twisted out of joint, lifted to the surface from the bowels of the island, and from there, from the surface, sent hurtling into the gaping chasms where the blown-up guns lay—a heap of burned and twisted metal.

Vibrations, as though from an earthquake, shook the island.

"They're blowing up the guns!" von Everscharp shouted. "They've violated the conditions of capitulation."

Just then the sun slowly entered a cloud bank. The cloud swallowed it. The red gloom which had enveloped the island and the sea faded away. Everything around took on a monotonous, granite-like hue. Everything—barring the flag on the church. Von Everscharp thought he was going crazy. In violation of all the laws of physics the enormous flag on the church spire continued to remain red. Standing out against the grey background its colour became more intense. It hurt the eye. Now von Everscharp understood everything. The flag had never been white. It had always been red. It could not have been anything else. Von Everscharp had forgotten whom he was fighting. This was no optical illusion. It was not the sun that had fooled von Everscharp. He had fooled himself.

Von Everscharp snapped out a new order.

A squadron of bombers, attacking planes and fighters took to the air. Torpedo boats, destroyers and invasion boats raced to the island from every side. New landing parties clambered up the wet cliffs. Parachutists dropped onto the roofs of the fishing village, looking for all the world like tulips. Explosions rent the air.

And amidst this inferno, making a last stand in the crypt under the church, thirty Soviet sailors trained their automatic rifles and machine-guns in the direction of all the four winds—south, east, north and west. In this last grim hour not one of them thought of life. That question had been settled. They knew that death awaited them. But, dying, they were determined to destroy as many of the enemy as possible. This was their fighting task. And they carried it out to the last.

The contending forces were too unequal.

Under a shower of brick and plaster torn out of the church walls by the dum-dum bullets, with their faces grimy from powder, drenched with blood and sweat, plugging their wounds with cotton wool torn from the lining of their tunics, the thirty Soviet sailors went down one after the other, fighting to the last breath.

Above them fluttered an enormous red flag sewn with big sailor's needles and coarse sailor's thread out of odd bits of red material, everything suitable that the sailors had found in their chests. It was sewn out of treasured silk handkerchiefs, red kerchiefs, crimson woollen scarves, pink tobacco pouches, vermillion blankets and jerseys. The blood-red calico backs ripped from the first volume of "The History of the Civil War" and two portraits—Lenin and Stalin, embroidered on cherry-coloured silk—presented to the fort by the young women of Kuibyshev—all went to make up this fiery mosaic.

At a dizzy height, amongst the scurrying clouds, it fluttered, waved, burned, as though some invisible gigantic standard bearer was impetuously carrying it through the smoke of the battlefield ever onwards to victory.

His Only Son

1

IT WAS far behind the lines. Fierce gusts of wind drove the snow and sleet over the ground. The scouts, having blown up the bridge, headed back towards the coast to the small, secluded cove where a motor launch should be waiting to take them off. After the first thaw the cliffs had become coated with ice and to scramble over them one had to go down on hands and knees. The Germans were tracking them in the snow with the tenacity of a pack of wolves, at times falling behind and losing the trail in the hills only to find it again.

Everything would have gone off splendidly had not Lieutenant Yermolov been wounded in the beginning by an automatic rifle burst fired at random—just that sheer bad luck which suddenly befalls people who have scores of times, smilingly, escaped death by a hair's breadth. Both Yermolov's legs were broken above the knee. He fell, raised himself on his elbows and asked for a drink A few drops were poured into his mouth from a flask. He looked at his crippled legs, at the dark pool of blood under him which was quickly staining the snow all around and said: "Leave me." They all knew that he was right but to leave him was simply beyond their power Captain Sergeyev, trying not to meet Yermolov's eyes, gave the order to lift him up and carry him. There were fifteeen of them. They carried Yermolov in turn, five at a time. When they came to a bit of steep ground they laid him down on the snow, then, while some of them scrambled to the top, those down below raised him on their arms and handed him up. Careful as they tried to be, their efforts availed but little.

They were moving much more slowly now and the Germans followed close behind. The men in the rear took cover behind boulders on the way and held them at bay with spurts from their light machine-guns. Two hours later their position grew serious. They were moving so slowly that the Germans, in all probability, had already caught up to them from the side.

It was while they were crossing a rift in the snow that Yermolov came for a moment out of his stupor. He called to the captain:

"Nearer. Come nearer," he said.

Sergeyev put his ear to the burning lips.

"You can't do things like that," Yermolov said. Although his words were scarcely audible the tone in which he spoke suddenly became firm and angry. "You can't do things like that. You'll ruin everything. It's downright treachery."

He stopped speaking and closed his eyes. He did not want to talk.

Sergeyev understood that the word "treachery" had been used deliberately, in order to force his hand, to compel him to do what Yermolov wanted. And what Yermolov wanted was, of course, right; it was dreadful, but right. Sergeyev left him and continued to walk alongside in silence. After they had crossed the rift, on the slope of a small hill strewn with rocks, he gave the order to put Yermolov down. They set him down on the snow, a shelter tent under him. Sergeyev ordered the others to go on ahead. He unbuckled the flask from his belt, took a tin of canned food from his knapsack and opened it with his knife. He placed the tin and the flask near Yermolov, just within reach of his left hand. After that he opened Yermolov's holster, took out his revolver and this, too, he laid down on the tent in such a way so that the wooden butt touched Yermolov's fingers.

Yermolov looked at him with submissive, unblinking eyes, but said nothing. He was reclining as though in an armchair, his back resting against the angle made by two boulders.

Sergeyev could now bear to look him in the eye. He had done everything, everything that was necessary, just as the dying man had wished.

"That's all," Sergeyev said. "Goodbye."

Yermolov took his hand and, without saying a word, shook it with a firmness entirely unexpected.

Sergeyev moved on, not turning even once to look back at him. A second later his white smock had disappeared behind a crag and Yermolov thought this was the last man he would see alive, barring, of course, the Germans.

He was suffering terribly from the pain. He wanted to put an end to it as quickly as possible, but the very thought of the Germans at once drove the idea of destroying himself out of his mind. He raised his revolver, cocked the hammer, and fired into the air. He did not want his comrades to undergo the torments of uncertainty: let them think that all was over, that this was the end. But he—he would still go on fighting. What overjoyed him was the easiness with which he had cocked the stiff hammer. He still had strength in his hands then—that was fine. He again raised the revolver and tried to take aim at a bit of moss that stuck out from under the snow. He sighted it easily, his hand did not shake. He lowered the revolver.

Snow was falling. Pale, snow-laden clouds overcast the sky. The Polar sun did not set but the dusk was darker than usual. With the instinct of a veteran scout he felt certain that, sooner or later, the Germans would pass him by, on the trail. The question now was at what distance would they spot him. At about thirty yards he would be able to score a hit. He looked with alarm at the sky: if only the snowstorm would keep on.

He was alone, all alone, nobody could help him, neither his comrades, nor even his oldest of all friends—his father. Closing his eyes he recalled his father as he had seen him last, in his dugout at army headquarters. He was poring over his artillery schedules, chewing the butt of a cigarette, and without raising his head had said in a grouchy tone that the scouts weren't doing their jobs properly—that during the last month they had spotted only four batteries. But in spite of the grouchy tone Yermolov knew that he had done his job well and that his father was satisfied with him, that he was grumbling just like that—that it was his way of hiding the love he felt for his only son.

And then his mind was suddenly crowded with disjointed, fleeting memories of trifling incidents in his friendship with his father. How his father had roundly abused him, did not feel at all sorry for him when, still a youngster, he had been thrown from his horse; how they had fenced together in the gym, in the artillery school in which his father had served at one time; how on one occasion he had forced his father into a corner and how pleased the old man had been and, for the first time, with a smile hidden under his moustaches, he had told his wife at dinner to place two wine glasses on the table, for the two men. He recalled how strict his father had always been to him, had never shown him the slightest affection, never once called him Alyosha but always the formal "Alexei," how he had always abused him in front of company and praised him but rarely, and then never to his face. And, yet, with all that poignancy of feeling which a man experiences who has but a few hours more to live, he sensed the intense love, tenderness and pride behind that long-standing, tranquil, even slightly cold

47

friendship with his father. He loved his mother, of course, yes, but just now he did not remember her loving hands, her tired smile, or the fine wrinkles under her eyes when she cried. All that seemed to him to be very far away just then and had nothing to do with what was happening to him at the moment. But the odd memories of his father were of vital importance to him now: they had a direct bearing on his lying here, with a revolver close at hand, and though he could hardly fight down the desire to put an end to the frightful pain his legs were causing him, still, despite everything, he would wait and go on waiting.

He, apparently, had decided to do what he was doing not only because this was the eleventh time he had gone out on scouting missions and was accustomed to the thought of a violent death, but because ever since a boy of four he had accompanied his father from barracks to barracks, from unit to unit, because his father had not been sorry for him when he had been thrown from his horse, because his father had been so pleased when he had forced him into a corner that time when they were fencing, and because his father, undoubtedly, could not imagine him dying in any other way than the way he wanted to just now.

He opened his eyes and glanced around. The snow was falling as heavily as before, his legs were entirely hidden under a white mound and the dark spots on the shelter tent could no longer be seen. For an instant it seemed to him that he was a small boy again, in bed, and that this was not snow but a white blanket and that his mother would come to him and draw it up to his shoulders and tuck him in. Loss of blood was evidently the cause of his becoming drowsy. It was a state of stupor which he had to overcome at all costs. Clenching his teeth, preparing himself for the inevitable pain, he mustered all his strength and suddenly jerked his leg. The frightful pain which for a moment had died down

48

shot through his whole body: the pain was something awful, as if somebody had driven a stake right through him. But he had achieved what he desired—the pain had shaken him out of the stupor.

He pricked up his ears. He heard a rustling to his right, from the opposite slope of the hill. "It's a good thing it's so soon," he thought and with his left hand he overturned the tin can and placed it under his right arm. Then, cocking his revolver, he rested his right elbow on the tin—it was higher and steadier like that.

The rustling became more audible. The Germans were moving rashly, very rashly. Splendid. But why was he alone, all alone? If only he had two of his men here armed with automatic rifles....

"It'll all be over in a minute and nobody will ever know how it happened, not a soul, not even Dad," he thought. "Dad, can you hear me?" was what he wanted to shout.

He rested his elbow more comfortably on the tin can and once again took aim to see whether he could sight the same bit of moss which was now barely perceptible in the snow.

The tracks led somewhat away from him, to the right, and the first German passed him by at a distance of about fifteen yards without even glancing in his direction. The second one, a dirty white tunic over his grey cavalry greatcoat and an automatic rifle slung around his neck, bent down to the path and, suddenly, glancing to the left, in his direction, let out a yell. Yermolov, his elbow pressing tightly against the tin can until it became painful, fired. The kick of the gun caused his weakened arm to slip off the tin. With difficulty he rested his elbow again on the tin and took aim at the second German who, hearing the yell and the thud of the falling body, turned in his direction. The German's automatic rifle got caught in the tape of his smock and Yermolov waited until he had torn it loose from around his neck. He fired only at the very last instant when the German, throwing his automatic rifle across his arm, was about to press the trigger. The rifle dropped from the German's hands; he stumbled on for a few paces, fell face down in the snow, right alongside, his hands almost touching Yermolov's legs.

Several shadows appeared simultaneously from the other side of the slope. Yes—precisely shadows. And because they were no longer human beings but dark spots which merged into a single whole, Yermolov understood that he was losing consciousness and that if he did not want to fall into their hands alive he must fire the last shot. In this last second he suddenly thought of his mother who had so often fondly caressed his face and his hair, and he pressed the revolver not to his temple but poked it under his unbuttoned jacket, about a couple of inches below the left pocket of his tunic. He clenched his fingers so tightly that his right hand, in its final convulsive movement, fell onto the snow, the revolver still gripped in it.

2

Colonel Yermolov returned to army headquarters only towards morning. Owing to the spring snowdrifts he had had to do the last twenty kilometres on foot and now, having pulled off his sodden boots, he was lying stretched out on his camp bed enjoying a smoke. The snowstorm, unusual for this time of the year, had been raging already for two days. The gusts of wind drove all warmth out of the dugout and the colonel, from time to time, got up in his bare feet in order to throw a log into the round iron stove. He had already reported to his superior officers the state of affairs at the forward positions; the commissar's bed was empty, he had not yet returned from divisional headquarters and an unusual silence reigned in the dugout, broken only from time to time by the crackling of the logs and the shrieking of the wind outside.

What previously, in the days of peace, had been regarded as loneliness—being parted from his dear ones, his wife and son, torn away from home—now, during the war, had long ceased to be regarded as such. The endless number of people who came to see him—Chief of Army Ordnance—at all hours, day and night, his commissar—a merry and shrewd Yaroslavite—with whom he had been sharing a roof for nearly eleven months, the commanders of his regiments, all of whom he recognized by their voices and rang up every night on the telephone —all this, which, on the whole, never left him a moment to spare the live long day and constituted his life, had long ago deprived him of a feeling of loneliness. But today, when the visibility from the observation posts had been reduced to nil owing to the snowstorm and everything would have to remain where it was until it had blown over, when, suddenly, for an hour, or even two, all necessity for telephone calls and even talking things over, here, at headquarters, had vanished, he, for some reason, could not fall asleep, and a loneliness. keener than he had ever experienced before, suddenly fell upon him.

He tried to picture his wife to himself. But she was somewhere so far away just then, in Siberia, that in his mind's eye all he could conjure up was a fleeting vision of an endless line of envelopes addressed in her hand, some of them still there, in Siberia, lying in a mail box, others on their way, in a mail train, others already somewhere very near, here, being sorted out at the post office by strange hands. They were all moving, coming towards him, but still they were only letters. and letters, however splendid, were after all only letters.

But his son was here. And, may be, just because he was here all the time, close at hand, the colonel just now so poignantly sensed this feeling of loneliness. He very rarely saw his son. At one time he had handed in a request through old friends that his son be assigned to the same army corps in which he himself was, and just because, contrary to his rule, he had once permitted himself to make such a request, he had never since gone out of his way to see his son more often than duty required. And duty required it rarely, very rarely. The last time he had seen him was a month ago, here—in this very dugout—when his son had reported the results of an artillery reconnoitring mission far behind the enemy's lines. The colonel had rejoiced at the time that his son had such a firm, manly face, that he was calm, terse and even a little over punctilious with him, his father. For the first time then he felt that his dear, clever, indulgent wife with whom he had argued so much on the subject had, nevertheless, not spoiled his only son, and that at twenty he found his boy just as he wanted him to be, yes, just as he wanted him to be, and just as he recollected himself when he was of the same age. He was even pleased that his son had refused the invitation to have tea with him and, drawing up to attention, had requested leave to go. He had given him permission but when his son had reached the door of the dugout the colonel had suddenly called to him:

"Alexei!"

And when his son turned round he had given him a wink, a friendly wink full of fun, just as when a youngster he had been guilty of some prank showing in him the traits of the future man. His son had winked back and with a smile still on his lips had repeated:

"May I go, Sir?"

And the colonel, also smiling, had again given him permission to go, and the boy had gone.

Such was their last meeting.

He had in fact a tender love for him and yearned for him as only fathers can yearn who have an only son, embodying their hopes, their pride, their faith that their child, their youngster, will in the long run grow up to be a real man—like themselves, or even better.

And just because he was ashamed of what in his opinion was his overweening love, the colonel never called his son anything but "Alexei," although to himself, in his thoughts, he was always "Alyosha" or "Alyoshka " It seemed to him at times that his son guessed this tender love of his, sensed it, and precisely at the very moment when he was being particularly strict with him.

It was again cold in the dugout. The colonel sat near the stove and began to throw some logs into it. The iron stove brought back memories of his youth—days when he was in command of a light-horse battery under Budyonny. Of late he had become accustomed to his staff duties and, on occasion, would laugh to scorn those of his subordinates who were overfond, without good reason, of poking into places where they had no right to be. But at times, at moments such as the present, he felt that he had been deprived of the direct feeling of coming to grips with the enemy, the flush of battle. Flitting memories passed through his mind of light guns drawn by teams of horses tearing over the ground, swinging around to take up a position and opening fire at short range, of gruff commands, sweaty faces of the gun crews, of men dressed in the uniform of the enemy sent crashing to the ground. Now he had been deprived of all this. The only time during the war when he had experienced this feeling, so reminiscent of the past, was yesterday and the day before yesterday. The army corps had taken the offensive and the chief observation post had been set up in a forward position on a high, rugged hill which had a commanding view of the whole area. On this occasion duty had not only permitted but demanded that he should be there, and so, for two whole days, he had personally directed the fire of several artillery units. These were batteries of the army corps' heavy guns and they bombarded at a long range the enemy's fortifications, emplacements and batteries. But from the hill one could see for such a long distance that through his field glasses he could make out, very faintly true, the scurrying figures of Germans, of horses going down and logs being blown sky-high.

His observation post had also come under the fire of first one and then another German battery; he had corrected the fire and fought them; and this feeling of a duel, of coming personally to grips, had pervaded him and his voice, when he snapped out an order, was gruff not only because of his cold and of the sleepless nights, but because of the flush of battle which held him thrilled.

But what had been yesterday and the day before yesterday had happened for the first time and might not happen again very soon. In this respect his son was more fortunate than he.

The colonel would never have admitted this to anybody, not even to his commissar, nor could he feel inclined to reproach himself. To him, from the standpoint of a father, the speciality of a scout which his only son had chosen was a very dangerous speciality. His son had not asked his approval, and he had acted rightly. What could he have said to him? Of course he would have approved. Even more, had his son requested a post under him, at staff headquarters, he would not only have been angry but he would have done everything in his power to prevent it. No, he did not despise staff work in general—that was stupid—but his son had to travel the same road he himself had travelled and he dare not skip a single stage on this road; to remain alive in the fulfilment of his duty depended on his son and only on his son—that was not his business, just as his son dared not encroach on those sleepless hours which he, his father, lived through at nights when the scouting parties were stranded for days on end somewhere in the enemy rear and there was no news of

54

them as was the case just now. As a matter of fact, truly and honestly, the reason why he could not fall asleep today was after all his son. There had been no news of the scouting party already for several days; a snow-storm was raging and nobody could say when it would end.

The colonel added the last log and sitting on his bed began to take off his belt in the vain hope of getting some sleep. Just then there was a knock on the door.

"Come in."

Captain Sergeyev, the commander of the scouting battalion, entered the dugout. He had evidently only just come back, he was still in his camouflage jacket, his automatic rifle was on his shoulder and he had no distinctive badges.

"What is it?"

"In a minute," Sergeyev replied, bringing down his automatic rifle with a clatter to the floor and sitting down on the commissar's bed.

Sergeyev was a taciturn man by nature. A glance at his face showed that he was dead beat, that he had just come back, and the fact that the artillery had given him no special assignment on his last reconnoitring expedition, his coming at this hour was both unexpected and alarming.

"What is it?" the colonel repeated and lighting a cigarette he moved along his bed so as to sit opposite Sergeyev, face to face.

"In a minute," Sergeyev repeated and for some reason he slowly pushed his automatic rifle away as though it hindered him from beginning the conversation.

"Is he wounded?" the colonel asked.

"No, Andrei Petrovich," Sergeyev said in a whisper. It was not so much the way he pronounced the word "no" but the fact that for the first time during all the months of war he addressed him so sympathetically, as though he were a sick man, by his name and patronymic, that the colonel understood that it was only a question of learning the details.

When Sergeyev had gone the colonel lay down flat on his bed, his face to the ceiling and tried to think. But his mind was a blank; one word kept running in his head, just one—"Alyosha," "Alyosha," "Alyosha"— the word he had never spoken out aloud while his son was alive. "Alyosha," he repeated, "Alyosha," and he again fell silent, closing his eyes, and again he opened them and endlessly repeated this one word. And still his mind was a blank, all that remained to him was his grief, to which it seemed to him he had so many times prepared himself during these long months of war, and yet had not succeeded. In order, somehow, to pull himself together he began to recall his conversation with Sergeyev. Why had he asked that pitiful and futile question: "Is there a note for me?" Of course there wasn't. Wouldn't have Sergeyev given it to him had there been one? But after all, why not? A couple of words at least.

And, suddenly, thinking of this note and the fact that there was no note he pictured to himself in all detail how it had happened: the shelter tent on the snow, the crippled legs of his son, the butt of the revolver Sergeyev had told him about, and that last shot he had heard when he was going away. No, no note was necessary. He, too, would not have written a note. Again he saw in his mind's eye his son's last road—the cliffs over which the motionless body had been carried on the shelter tent, the rocks on which he had been left lying alone, all alone, or no—together with his weapon, his revolver—the soldier's last mate in life. He saw his cold body and the Germans who approached him. Germans.... Half an hour ago Captain Sergeyev had deliberately, as though trying somewhat to mitigate his grief, recalled at length the scouting expeditions in which he had taken part, together with his son, the hand grenades sent flying into the enemy's bunkers, the bridges that had been blown up, the German officers they had wiped out. No, it had not mitigated his grief. It was his only son and now, when he was dead, nothing in the world could replace his loss. But the thought that his son had succeeded, had nevertheless succeeded in settling his score for himself, prevented his grief from turning into despair though it remained a grief.

Involuntarily he thought of himself during these last days, the scurrying soldiers he had observed through his field glasses, the horses going down, the logs blown sky-high, and it seemed to him just then that in the ferocity of this battle in which he had taken part during these latter days there was a foreboding, as it were, of the death of his son, a foreboding of the vengeance that was his, the bereaved father.

It seemed to him that at those moments, when he was snapping out orders in a gruff voice at the observation post, that he was next to his son and that together... they were demolishing, destroying, killing these men whom he hated so intensely that he was ready to choke the lives out of them.

But he did not feel any the better for all that. He realized just then that he could never give way to hopelessness, to despair, that just as before, in spite of the grief that he had to bear, he just as vehemently wanted to live and fight, yes, mainly, to fight.

But his wife? What would she say.... She could not choke the lives out of these murderers with her own hands, she could not, as he, direct the long muzzles of his death-dealing guns. To write to her, tell her that her boy had left his last bullet for himself—no that was impossible. To tell her that his comrades could not lower her boy's body into the grave—was also impossible. He realized that his grief would not pass, neither tomorrow nor the day after tomorrow—never, that he must write to her at once, right now, at this table, not putting it off till tomorrow, because tomorrow it would be still harder than today. He would write to her at once. May she forgive him for the lie he'd tell her, for in telling her the truth about what was most vital and terrible he could not but withhold the truth as to the rest.

When he had finished his letter the grey imperceptible spring night had already come to an end. He went out of his dugout. Above the snowstorm, above the hilltops, a cold sun was rising. From the west came the heavy thunder of guns. He looked at his watch: yes, it was exactly eight. It was his guns firing, the artillery offensive had begun—the very offensive which he had timed yesterday evening for eight this morning when he had not yet known that he no longer had a son.

The guns opened fire punctually at eight—just as it should be. The war went on.

Snowbound

1

HE USUALLY began the day with a rub down and this
morning too Sviridov stripped to the waist, sponged
his face, neck, chest and as much of his back as he
could reach, did a few exercises to ease his taut muscles,
dried himself, slipped into his things and forgot about his
dream.

Sitting down to breakfast, however, in the dugout
where the commanders messed, Sviridov thought to himself:

"There's no doubt about it, the things people do must
be really bewildering to the wild creatures in the swamps
and woods!... Scouring the land and air, poking into the
most out of the way places—what is there left for them
to do? Only one thing remains: to clear out of harm's
way as quickly as possible!"

That day he was assigned to do patrol duty over that
far range of hills that loomed blue in the distance and
from behind which enemy bombers usually attempted to
break through to Murmansk.

The flying field where his plane stood carefully camou-
flaged in line with others, was covered with a soft layer
of snow which was not deep enough though to hinder
the machines from taking off or making a landing.

Dressed warmly for the flight Sviridov, from a distance,
seemed big and clumsy; although as a matter of fact, he

was lithe and supple and a splendid athlete. He left the dugout taking with him, as usual, an emergency packet containing some tins of canned food and several bars of chocolate. Together with Lieutenant Badikov, his ground mechanic, he got the machine ready for the flight and shortly after, the plane, leaving a broad track as it ran lightly over the snow, took off and began to soar skywards.

It so happened that Sviridov forgot to give Badikov the usual "Cheerio" when he climbed into the cockpit. He remembered it only when the plane was taking off. "It doesn't matter," he thought.... "After all, I won't be up for long.... I'll be back today."

He had often gone up on patrol duty and come back within the stipulated time without encountering anybody in the air. But early that morning he, like the other men, had felt certain that it was going to be a day for flying. The sky, it was true, was overcast but here and there were big patches of pale blue. And when the plane, gathering altitude, cut through two layers of clouds, the horizon widened and became much clearer.... Suddenly, Sviridov noticed the dim silhouettes of three planes lurking behind some clouds.

"Maybe they're our planes, not fascist?" he thought.

The plane, answering the experienced hand on the controls, headed for the spot.

Sviridov simply wanted to make sure that they were really friendly planes. He was almost certain at first that they were. But the nearer he drew the clearer it became that they were not—that they were enemy planes.

From the ground he would have recognized them at once by the characteristic sound of their engines but now the roar of his own drowned out everything else. What gave the enemy away was their yellow camouflage. His eyes sought for the white disk with the black swastika in the centre on the nearest plane and he found it. And immediately he decided to attack them.

But in order to do so he had to gain altitude. The plane began to climb. Minutes passed, minutes which seemed to drag on eternally so keen was Sviridov on riddling the enemy plane as quickly as possible with a long burst from his machine-gun.

His chance came. The nearest bomber was the leader of the unit. Swooping down, Sviridov opened fire, riddling the right wing.

The heavy machine disappeared in a cloud of smoke and began to lose altitude.

"Take that, you swine!" Sviridov shouted with glee. "That's kaput for you!"

Whether it crashed or managed to make a landing somewhere that bomber was out of action anyway. But how about the other two?

He kept his eyes on them. Without their leader, he saw, they began to veer away from their set course—and most interesting of all—were trying to make tracks as quickly as their engines permitted them.... His supply of ammunition gave out.

"Ram them!" This was the command that Sviridov seemed to give himself as he directed his plane to intercept the nearer one.

"No, you don't, you skunk! You won't get away so easily!" the Lieutenant thought, spurring himself on as it were and noticeably reducing the distance that separated him from the nearer enemy plane.

The German bomber he had just brought down was his sixth; the one ahead of him would be the seventh. One of the first five he had also rammed, only just slightly denting his own screw in doing it. In his mind's eye he already saw this one, too, which was trying to get away from him, added to his score of rammed planes.

He was so sure of success that what actually did happen was something entirely unexpected.

Whether it was he who made a slight but fatal mistake when, hovering over the tail of the German plane he was preparing to strike it full blast, or whether the German flier, in some fraction of a second veered slightly to the left, but, anyhow, when the screw of his plane hit the tail of the German plane and bits of the rudder went hurtling down, Sviridov felt that the left wing of his own plane had also been damaged: it had crashed against the rudder of the German plane.

The force of the impact almost threw Sviridov out of his seat. His plane trembled in every fibre—this had not happened on the first occasion when he had rammed a German plane. And although the Lieutenant saw that the enemy bomber was hurtling to the ground, still he derived but small satisfaction therefrom. He felt that his own machine too, quivering and rocking, was veering to the left and losing altitude. He realized that his left wing had been badly damaged, that to go on with the flight or try to reach his own aerodrome was out of the question, that he would be lucky if he could land his plane somewhere and in such a way so as not to cripple it for good and bury himself under the wreckage.

The momentary shock which had made him go hot and cold passed, leaving him calm and collected; the slightest mistake on his part now spelled death. He had to land his machine somewhere, but, where? Below, as far as his eye could see, stretched a range of rugged hills, steep cliffs that rose almost perpendicular and were therefore devoid of snow. These granite rocks made the ground appear striped, like an enormous mattress. There was no time to pick and choose a landing place; the plane could still glide down, but to fly was out of the question.

Sviridov was so engrossed with the thought of saving the machine and, consequently, of saving himself, that he completely forgot about the bomber he had just rammed. He felt indifferent as to which hilltop it had crashed on. He was indeed overjoyed when he suddenly noticed an even patch of ground in a cleft in the hills. He did not grasp at first that it was a frozen lake covered over with snow; the only thing he saw was that it was a suitable place to make a landing. The wheels of the plane skimmed over the snow, ran on for a couple of dozen yards or so, and came to a stop.

The snow lay uneven; in some places it was deep, in others it barely covered the ground. He switched off the engine. Silence reigned. The one thought in his mind now was that he was alive, that his machine was intact, that it could be repaired and would fly again. What he had to do now was to take a look round, fix the place in his memory and figure out the best and quickest way of getting back to his own aerodrome.

Sviridov pushed back his goggles onto his forehead, unstrapped his parachute, opened the sliding hood of the cockpit and looked out.

The lake was hemmed in by hills, but the slopes, overgrown with trees and shrubs, were not very steep. The dips in the hills where the snow seemed to be particularly deep stood out like indigo. One could hardly imagine human beings anywhere in the vicinity, so profound was the silence.

But suddenly, a shot rang out breaking the silence. It was so unexpected that Sviridov could hardly believe his ears—was it a shot or was it the ice cracking?... But two or three seconds later another shot rang out and a bullet even seemed to patter against the plane. Sviridov drew his revolver and taking a firm grip of it leant out.

The first thing he saw was a huge dog—a mouse-coloured wolf-hound; the two German fliers lumbering behind it he noticed the next instant, and only after that did he catch sight of the bomber so recently rammed by him: the German pilot had landed it at the other end of the same lake.

He had to deal with two enemies and an enormous dog which they had taken it into their heads to bring along with them. The dog was already quite near, bounding clumsily towards him through the snow. But it was not at the dog that Sviridov fired three times in succession but at the nearest German who was shooting as he ran. When he picked him off the dog was only two or three yards away. Sviridov just managed to lean back in the cockpit and close the hood.

The dog growled and began scraping the hood of the cockpit with its paws. Its ears lay flat on its broad square head; its hair bristled. Vicious green eyes, enormous white fangs, foam around the snarling mouth, a growl which grew into a bark, and the big, husky German rushing up behind—all this he observed through the window of his cockpit.

The dog made an attempt to leap onto the smooth surface of the plane but finding no foothold went sprawling on its back into the snow. Acting on the spur of the moment Sviridov opened the sliding hood, leant over the side and fired. The enormous animal fell writhing, staining the snow with its blood. It could not get up—it had a bullet through its head. With its long tongue it licked up the snow.

The German, a heavy, broad-shouldered fellow with a bloated face and green eyes, seemed to be the very image of his dog. Now he was very near.

"You wait, you Russian swine, I'll get you!" he shouted in Russian.

The threat in Russian was so unexpected that Sviridov was out of the cockpit in a flash making for the German.

He fired at him but he was so furious that he could not make out whether the shot went wide or whether he only slightly wounded him; the German, growling like a dog, muttering: "I'll get you," sent him sprawling on his back, pinning him down by the sheer weight of his heavy body.

Sviridov mustered all his strength, and, although his leather coat hindered his movements, managed to throw off the German. But in doing so his revolver slipped out of his hand. The next minute the German had him down again and gripped him by the throat with both hands.

Sviridov's strength was going fast, he could scarcely breathe but, drawing in his left shoulder he wrenched his right from under the German. The German let go and Sviridov, filling his lungs with the fresh cold air, remembered about his revolver and began to grope around for it in the snow.

The German, however, forestalled him. He had let go his hold in order to unsheath a knife from his belt, and what an exultant look gleamed in his round, green, doggish eyes as he slashed at Sviridov's face, ripping up the left cheek from the bridge of the nose to the lower jaw.

An agonizing pain seemed to shoot through the Lieutenant—to his very marrow. A knife in the hand of his foe—that was sure death.... He remembered his grandfather once saying to him: "If some roughneck gets the better of you, kick him between the legs!" Sviridov drew up his right foot and making one final effort hit the German between the legs with his knee.

The German shouted with pain and bent double. His hand, with the knife in it, raised for a second—this time fatal—blow, fell limply to his side. Sviridov in the meantime had found his revolver buried under him in the snow. Without losing a second he fired in the direction the muzzle pointed—the bullet lodged in the German's left side. At once he felt that he was free: his enemy slid off his chest; Sviridov wriggled to one side and sat up, too weak to get onto his feet.

He sat like that for several minutes looking into the open, glazed eyes of his mortal enemy, then stretching out his hand for some clean snow he pressed it against the gaping wound on his face; when one handful of snow became crimson with his blood he threw it away and took another.

The dog ceased jerking its legs convulsively and lay still. The first German also lay dead in the snow about thirty yards away. And standing motionless, one facing the other, just as at an aerodrome, were two planes—one with a swastika on it and the other with a Red Star.

A vast stillness hung over the icy lake, in the surrounding hills, in the overcast sky. The sole human creature here now was he, Lieutenant Sviridov, with a deep knife gash extending down the length of his face.

2

The pain was intolerable—a gnawing pain which made his head swim.

To close his lips was impossible. The entire upper gum on the left side of his face was slashed open as well as a part of the lower one. For a long time he sat there spitting out blood.

But it was time to be up and going and, without losing a moment, start out in the direction of his own camp: the winter day was short everywhere, but here, in the tundra, it was shorter than anywhere else.

Sviridov went up to his plane and took what he thought he would need most on the way: his emergency packet, map and compass. He reloaded his revolver, took a last look around at his own plane and at the enemy's, at the bodies of the Germans and then set off due north for the sea.

He had to negotiate deep snow in one place, scale the bare icy slope of the steep granite hill in another, manœuvre creeper trees which more resembled bushes. He had hardly topped the summit when dusk fell.

He had been almost certain that from here, from the top of such a high hill, he would be able to see the dark strip of sea just as he had many a time before from his plane. But the only thing that met his eyes was another range of hills which loomed dark in the distance.

He tried mentally to recall his course from the begin-

66

ning of the flight up to the time when he encountered the German bombers and then the direction he had taken after that, so as to determine his approximate whereabouts now on the ground. But he could not remember a thing. Other matters had crowded it out of his mind. The map he had with him was useless: all it showed here was a white spot.

Plodding along he did not feel the cold and when the day was finally over he decided to call a halt and sat down in the snow. He was dead beat after his tussle with the Germans, weak from loss of blood and from the walk, but when he tried to fortify his strength somewhat with the chocolate he had in his emergency packet he found that he could not eat. The pain in his mouth made it impossible for him to clench his teeth which, moreover, were very loose. He held a bit of chocolate on his tongue for a while and then spat it out.

He knew that the night would not be dark, that the sky in the North would be aglow with the northern lights; and the northern lights did appear in their usual way, suddenly rending the dark sky with lights all the colours of the rainbow. From here, from the top of the barren hill, the display created a much grander impression than from there, from his dugout, but still no less incomprehensible. It appeared spontaneously, a purposeless phenomenon when, around, everything seemed to answer the needs of the war: the sky—to fly, the ground—to dig trenches, the sea—to carry naval transports and vessels.

The hue of the snow-capped hills changed from blue to rose, with splashes of light like golden corn, and Sviridov watched this play of iridescence as though in some art gallery. Gradually, however, his eyelids grew heavy with sleep and he fell into a doze, his back against a boulder.

He was dozing, not sleeping, because while his mind seemed to be engulfed in a dark abyss some section of

5*

his brain kept him conscious that he was on a hill, that he was alone, that around him was a snow-swept waste, that the night dragged on, that the aurora borealis kept up its dancing columns of light.

He woke up with a start, jerking his head back; something had grazed his wounded face causing him unbearable pain. He even raised himself somewhat to look around.

Not far away, on the edge of a cliff, he noticed two gleaming pin-points quite close to each other; they had not been there before. They vanished for a moment and then reappeared. He guessed that they were the eyes of an owl, a big, white Polar owl, and that the owl, probably, had flitted by so closely that it had grazed his face with its wing and, maybe, had even alighted on his shoulder.

And then the silence was broken by a shrill call: another owl flitted by overhead and alighted not far from the first one. Making a snowball he threw it in the direction of the two pairs of gleaming eyes. The owls flew away; their calls could be heard in the distance.

Sviridov got up and continued on his way. However, the northern lights which provided sufficient light when walking over even ground thinly covered with snow, here, on the hillsides, proved very deceptive owing to the irregular and rapid change of colour. The Lieutenant suddenly found himself almost up to his waist in snow when he imagined he was on firm ground and went barging into trees when he thought he had carefully skirted their sharply defined shadows.

After an hour or so he decided to give it up and sat down to wait for dawn. Again he dozed off; and again the white owls hovered silently over him. Driving them off with snowballs he recollected a certain incident at his flat in Moscow.

Nura used to keep some of the food on the balcony in winter. After a while she noticed that pats of butter, or ham cut up in slices and covered with a plate, would every now and then disappear—and on one occasion a chicken she had prepared for the next day's dinner had been simply rent to pieces.

The blame was put on somebody's prowling cat, although it was a mystery how a cat could reach their balcony on the sixth floor. One day she happened to chance on a crow on the balcony. From Nura's description it was an unusually big crow and one, apparently, very experienced in making thieving raids of this kind. The butter, for instance, it removed neatly from the paper wrapper; it pushed the plate off with its beak to get at the ham, doing it carefully so as not to make a noise, and in the case of the chicken—only the liver and the heart were taken. . . .

He mused about his Moscow flat, Nura and Katya. . . . He pictured to himself how Lieutenant Badikov and his other comrades had waited and waited for him to come back and had, of course, decided by now that he was dead.

His eyelids grew heavy, he slept fitfully, the owls shrieked, the northern lights danced on the round summits of the hills—and in this way the night passed. With the first streaks of daylight he continued on his way setting his course by compass.

It seemed to him that the sea must be somewhere not very far away, that in an hour or two, or three at the most, he would see it. He wanted to believe it and he made himself believe it. But the further he went the more difficult it became to drag his benumbed feet.

He understood that he must eat something although, as a matter of fact, he did not feel very hungry yet. But when he took the bar of chocolate out again and placed a bit in his mouth he became convinced that he could not possibly chew it or even suck it. The pain was more than he could bear, and he threw away the whole bar in the snow.

He did it in disgust but later on it was not a feeling

of disgust but the enormous burden of everything he had on and with him that induced him to throw away the two tins of preserves from his emergency packet; they were absolutely useless to him just now—after all he couldn't eat them and they were so terribly heavy.

Whether he only imagined it was so or had to convince himself that what he had done was the right thing —but for a while he walked on more briskly.

He stopped near a spring which trickled out from under the thin ice and disappeared in the snow and began to drink from the palm of his hand. To swallow was painful but he was extremely thirsty and the cold water refreshed his mouth. He sat near the spring for over an hour and made two or three attempts to drink.

He had not gone very far when he was startled to see the dog. There it was not very far away, come to life again, or so it seemed to him at first sight—the big, mouse-coloured German dog—pacing along slowly about ten yards away through the swirling snow.

The Lieutenant's hand crept towards his holster. Suddenly he noticed the sharply pointed ears and bushy tail and understood that it was a wolf.

The big wolf trod so lightly that its paws hardly left a trace in the snow, and it kept its eyes on him in a way that seemed to be quite good-natured. Sviridov strode on, the wolf almost at his side, just like two old friends. At first the Lieutenant did not consider it at all unpleasant.

True, he knew nothing about the habits of the Polar wolves, but from childhood he had heard people say about the wolves in the Ryazan district where he came from that they did not attack human beings. He stopped several times to let the wolf by, but the wolf stopped too.

Though somewhat refreshed at first by the cold water Sviridov again began to give way to fatigue. He was almost certain that he had a high temperature; he felt gnawing pains all over his body. It was then that the

Lieutenant realized that the wolf was following him not for nothing, that the brute sensed how feeble the man was, that at any moment he would drop not to rise again. Then he would become its lawful prey.

Sviridov stopped. The wolf looked at him and sat down on its haunches, turning its head away as though out of decency.

Sviridov slowly pulled out his revolver. "How heavy it's become," he muttered to himself. And just as slowly he raised the gun and pulled the trigger. He did not take aim. He fired only to scare the wolf away and, indeed, frightened by the shot it dashed away and disappeared somewhere amongst the hills.

A snowstorm began in real earnest. And worst of all it started towards evening. The hope of catching sight of the sea was what had kept him going so far but now the swirling snowflakes driving in his face hid everything from sight. It grew terribly cold.

He found a spot where he could sit with his back to the wind and when it grew quite dark and the millions of snowflakes sparkled and gleamed with the iridescence of the northern lights, he felt sorry for himself that he was destined to freeze to death there.

He could hardly keep awake, but to go to sleep would be taking too great a risk. He knew that it was while asleep that people froze to death; first sleep would take them in its arms and then death. He tried to persuade himself that he was too warmly clad to freeze to death but at the same time he felt that he was shivering all over.

When he left the plane he was under the impression that before long he would get back to camp and then fly back to the lake accompanied by Badikov and some others; that his plane would be repaired and would again soar through the air and that, perhaps, they would also manage to repair the German bomber. Now he was afraid the Germans would get to the lake before him.

His lacerated gums seemed to be paining him more than ever: every one of his teeth ached. The slightest shadow in front of him or to one side of him he took for the wolf that had come back: there it sat watching, waiting, whether the man was still alive, whether it was possible to dig its fangs into his body, its enormous white fangs, just like the fangs of that dog.

He remembered now quite clearly the dream he had had the other night, the last night he spent in his dugout: a crested lark, its eyes red with terror, frantically beating its wings. He could hear its plaintive voice: "I'm a lark. ... I can speak like a human being. ... But people want to roast me!" And then for some inexplicable reason Katya was on his lap and she was asking him endless questions about larks and how they sing. ... He pressed his wounded cheek against her soft hair and the pain ceased.

Several pairs of owls' eyes gleamed here and there but whether he actually saw them or only imagined them, Sviridov was not sure. But instinctively he felt almost certain that owls were sitting somewhere nearby, that they had come here together with the snowstorm, that they remembered—were bound to remember—him since last night, that just like the wolf they could not allow their prey to get away.

The blizzard raged all night long. Sviridov was amazed to see how the storm abated with the first signs of the coming dawn, lost its force and died down. ... When it was light enough to make out the hands of his compass he started out again.

The storm had piled up the snow in some places, in others it had swept the ground bare, making it difficult to walk, or so it seemed to him; actually he was ready to collapse at any moment. The night's rest had braced him up somewhat, but not for long. His leather coat weighed heavily on his shoulders. ... Hardly able to drag his feet along he wondered what he could throw away into the snow so that it would be easier for him to walk. But what? The revolver? He couldn't do that—the wolf might turn up again.... His compass? He couldn't do that either, otherwise he would never reach the sea.... He searched through his pockets and found a pencil. Here was something that was useless to him now. He threw it away.

He tottered on as though in a daze, dragging his heavy legs along, moving somehow, peering at times into the distance, in the direction where the sea should be. And when towards evening he finally did come in sight of the sea he was so weak that it left him totally indifferent. Almost at the same instant he noticed the dim shape of a man—the only man he had seen for several days—and the first thing he did was to draw out his terribly heavy revolver.

Since the last people he had seen were German fliers who had been bent on killing him, it seemed to him through the mist swimming in front of his eyes that this one, too, was a German. A minute later, losing consciousness from sheer fatigue, he was in the capable hands of a sailor of the Northern Fleet, while three others came running up to lend a hand.

NIKOLAI TIKHONOV

The Duel

THE GERMAN pilot could distinctly see his prey. Through the forest, that from above looked like a green pie, ran a narrow yellow strip. It was a railway embankment, and along it crawled a military freight train. There was no sense in swooping down on it while it was in the forest. He had only to wait until it reached the clearing between this forest and the next, and he could bomb it unerringly and at leisure.

The plane swung round. Its wings glistened in the sun. It circled round once more, climbed, and then dived down towards the clearing. Two columns of mud and earth spouted up on either side of the embankment where the train should have been. But when the pilot looked down he saw that on reaching the clearing the train had suddenly backed into the forest again. The bombs had been wasted.

The German circled once more. He was determined that this time he would not miss his mark. The train was speeding across the clearing. How could its driver know that the reception was now awaiting him in the forest and that the heavy pines, uprooted and blown sky-high by the thunderous explosion, would come crashing down on to the freight cars? The pines fell, but without doing any damage. The train had slipped past them. Again the bombs had been wasted.

The pilot cursed furiously. Was this long, clumsy goods train going to get away scot free? The German

74

swooped down on the forest, aiming at the very middle of the train. Perhaps he had miscalculated, perhaps it was a mere chance, but the bombs fell wide of their mark. The elusive train was continuing to speed forward on its course, puffing indomitably.

"Steady now!" the pilot said to himself. "This time I'll let him have it in real earnest." He studied the ground carefully and made his calculations with calm deliberation. This unusual hunt was beginning to fascinate him.

Once more he swooped down to that spot on the ground where the transparent ribbon of smoke wavered in the vibrating air. It seemed to him that he was diving right into the locomotive. But at the last moment it seemed as if somebody had snatched the train away from under his wings. The roar of the explosion was still ringing in his ears when the conviction was brought home to him that he had missed once again. He glanced down. That was so! The train was gliding forward absolutely unimpaired.

The German realized that he was up against a will no less stubborn than his own, that the engine-driver had the eye of a hawk and an astonishing faculty for precise calculation, and that it would be no easy matter to catch him.

The duel continued. Bombs fell in front of the train, behind it, and on either side, but the monster, as the pilot called it, continued on its way to the station, as though protected by invisible spirits.

The train hopped and leaped fantastically. Its couplings shrieked frantically. It took the inclines like a horse with the bit between its teeth, and put on the brakes just when the next shower of bombs was awaiting it. It backed, it stopped, it shot forward like an arrow. There seemed to be no end to the tricks which this exasperating monster could play in the hands of its driver. The bombs burst like squibs.

The German was sweating profusely. He spat in disgust. He flung himself into the attack again and again. The last time he calculated perfectly. There was no escape for the train now. For the first time the engine-driver had, in his opinion, made a mistake. But an oath broke from the pilot's lips. He had used up all his bombs.... He had nothing to send hurtling down at the train!

He soared down, flying low over the train and peppering it from his machine-gun. But as luck would have it, another stretch of forest appeared. The train plunged into its green seclusion and it seemed that it was invulnerable. The pilot was frantic. He aimed at the locomotive, at the enemy lurking behind that thin wall, at that diabolical Russian working man who was scoffing at him, a brave German ace, and driving his train like mad across fields and through forests....

Bullets rained down on to the train. Some found a mark under its wheels, others struck the rails, making them ring, but the train kept persistently on its way....

The German leaned back exhausted. The sky glistened overhead. It was a serene, crystal-clear autumn day, reminding him of the autumns of his far-off Westphalia.

His supply of ammunition had come to an end. The duel was over. That Russian down below had won.

What should he do? Ram the locomotive? Answer madness with madness? A shiver ran down the pilot's back. He lowered his plane and sailed over the train in a fit of curiosity and hatred. He could not see that the keen eyes of the driver were following him. All the driver said was:

"Diddled you this time, you skunk!"

And the locomotive, in contempt, ran over and crushed the shadow sprawling across the track—the shadow of the enemy plane.

A Child Is Born

THE MAN stood panting heavily. He was angry and at a loss.

"I had the devil of a job finding you. It's so dark that a man could walk past his own house without knowing it," he said, shaking the snow from his cap. "Is this the lying-in hospital?"

"It is," he was told. "What's the matter?"

"What's the matter? Why, a woman is giving birth in a backstreet. That's what's the matter."

"And who are you?"

"I just happened to be passing by. I was on my way home from the night shift. Come on, let's get going. I'll show you the way. A fine business!... I was walking along, and there she was, and not a soul about except myself.... What could I do? I'm not a midwife."

A minute later Irina, a probationary nurse and the stranger were stumbling through the snowdrifts. It was pitch dark. The houses stood like sheer cliffs. Not a light was to be seen. Along the street swept a blizzard and snow dust whirled through the air. And it seemed as if the shadows of scouts were stealing through the street, transparent, frigid and swift-moving.

Suddenly, they squatted down in the snow, their noses buried in each other's backs. A thin, evenly rising sound was heard, drawing closer and closer. They drew their heads down between their shoulders. Somewhere from around the corner red flames shot upwards and a deafening explosion reverberated through the street. Icicles dropped from the eaves and smashed to bits on the pavement with a tinkling sound.

"She hasn't been hit I hope!" Irina exclaimed.

"No, she's on the other side. Look for her over there," said the stranger. "You'll find her beyond the lamp-post. I'm off. The shooting is fierce tonight. There's no sense in my hanging around."

Irina was not a midwife by training. She was a nurse in the reception room of the lying-in hospital. But now she had to go out into the night to search for this woman and help her in childbirth. There was no time to lose. Nobody else would come to her aid. It was the dead of night, a bitterly cold, wind-swept night and the city was being bombarded. With a hiss and a clang, shell after shell passed overhead. Irina and the probationer ran from snowdrift to snowdrift, stopped and listened.

A groan came from somewhere on the right. They dashed to the spot and, sure. enough, beyond the lamppost, just as the stranger had said, huddled up with her back against the wall of a house near the locked and barred gates, sat a woman in the snow. Irina dropped on her knees before her, and the woman seized her hand in her own. It was hot and trembling.

Yes, it was too late to bring this woman to the lying-in hospital. She was already in the throes of childbirth. She was bearing her child in the snow, in that black winter's night, illuminated by the fitful glare of bursting shells. Irina glanced around. It all looked like a gloomy nightmare. The snow penetrated under the collar of her coat down her neck, fierce gusts of wind drove the snow in her face, her hands grew numb with the cold, and her heart throbbed so violently that she could hear its beat. It seemed as if there were no Leningrad, but only a wild, black wilderness, swept by a blizzard and the barking of enemy guns. It would be useless to hammer at those locked and barred gates, it would be useless to call for help—the street was deserted, and until morning came no human being would pass that way.

Yet here, in this gloom, in this open spot, swept by all the four winds, a new life was coming into being. It had to be saved, it had to be snatched from the cold and the murk and the guns. Her ear was already deaf to the roar of the guns and the exploding shells. She helped the woman as if she were lying in a snug ward,

in the way women are always helped in childbirth...

...She raised the infant high in the air, as if to
display it to the great city lying lost in the gloom. She
carried it tightly clutched to her bosom, this warm, whim-
pering mite, nestling beneath her coat. She strode through
the snow, which was fresh and still untrod by human feet.

Behind her, supported by the attendant, like some
large ruffled bird, the mother dragged her weary feet. She
stumbled in the snowdrifts. She whispered through her
parched lips: "I'll manage myself...." The probationer,
herself tired and worried, merely kept reiterating: "We'll
be there soon; it's not very far now...."

The blizzard drove handfuls of dry snow into their
faces. A rain of shatterd glass followed on each thunder-
ing explosion. But they strode forward like conquerors,
conquerors of the night, the cold, and the cannonade. Had
there been need this procession would have marched through
the whole city, carrying this new tiny life, this new tiny
being, which had appeared in our city in this amazing hour.

The mother already knew that she had given birth to
a girl. Now and again she would stretch her hands out
towards Irina who was carrying the infant, as though she
wanted to stay her, and then let them fall again.

They arrived at the lying-in hospital. And when the
woman had already been put to bed, and everything was
being done to make her comfortable, she called for Irina
and asked her in a curt, almost stern whisper:

"What is your name?"

"Why do you want to know?" asked Irina.

"I must know."

"My name is Irina. But why do you ask?"

"I shall call my daughter after you. Let her remember you. You saved her life. I thank you from the bottom of my heart...."

And she kissed her three times. Irina turned away and
burst into tears. Why, she could not say.

Spring

THE HOUSE was in a terribly neglected state. It had withstood air raids during which bursting bombs had in some places shattered the windowpanes and blown out the window frames; it had seen direct hits from shells which had set fire to a part of the attic and the top floor. During the winter it had become littered with rubbish, the water pipes had burst, the baths and the washstands were covered with dirty ice, snow and muck were piled up on the balconies, the floors were dented in places where people had chopped wood on the parquet in the winter, the walls were grimy and, in general, there was a cold and musty air in every corner.

They had set to work repairing it without any outside help, tackling the job energetically, vigorously. Nobody thought of enlisting Ivan Nikolayevich. He would have been surprised if he—the surgeon—had been suddenly requested to become a plain and ordinary navvy. The house could be repaired and used for a hospital; it was a strong, sturdy building, but to set it to rights required an enormous amount of work. Everybody had their hands full, particularly the commissar, who did not have a minute's rest the day round.

The house was like a beehive. In one place carpenters were busy at work, in another—house painters. But actually they were neither carpenters nor house painters. The hospital staff—doctors, nurses, attendants and orderlies —rolling up their sleeves, scraped, washed, planed, painted and cleaned up. The hum of the city drifted in through the open windows: the tingling of the first street cars started with the winter over, the hooting of cars, the distant droning of planes patrolling the sky, the rumbling of heavy artillery.

That morning Ivan Nikolayevich asked one of the nurses who was smeared from head to foot with plaster:

"Where can I find Doctor Katonin, please?"

She directed him. It took him a long time to make his way up several flights of broad stairs and then up a narrow staircase with a black, cold banister, until, finally, he reached the roof. It was a big flat roof with a summer-house at one end. It gave an excellent view of quite a large section of the city. Here and there spires towered above a sea of red roofs. The distant horizon—a greenish blue—evidenced that spring had come. The roof was littered with ice-coated rubbish from which bits of boards and other junk protruded.

Doctor Katonin, armed with a pick, was hacking away at this dirty green ice-locked pile. Chips of ice were flying in all directions. The doctor did not even once glance round and Ivan Nikolayevich watched him in silence dealing hefty blows. After a while Katonin straightened his back, thrist the pick into the ice and, rubbing his hands, turned round. Without showing the least sign of surprise he looked at Ivan Nikolayevich and said:

"Here's an interesting job, colleague, damn it all. Anyhow, we've got to clear this mess away and as quickly as possible. After all we'll have to live and work here...."

He spat on his hands and with the frenzy of an old miner again set to work breaking up the ice. Ivan Nikolayevich, his hands behind his back, looked first at him and then at the city stretched out below. He looked at it intently as though seeing it for the first time. As a matter of fact he had more than once been on this roof. Years ago there used to be a restaurant here, a jolly, lively place....

Katonin was hacking away for all he was worth oblivious to everything else. Ivan Nikolayevich left the roof on tiptoe. The lines on his forehead were more marked than usual and his shoulders twitched nervously.

The next day he went to the works office and pointing to a distant corner where various instruments were lying around, he said to the superintendent:

"Give me that thing over there... what d'ye call it, a

crowbar I think, or a shovel or a rake, or any old thing so long as it'll be handy to clear the roof...."

"But your hands, doctor," the superintendent said. "Is it worth while? We'll get along somehow without you."

"What?" Ivan Nikolayevich shouted. "Don't worry about my hands, I'll look after them myself. Here, give me a tool of some kind. I've talked it over with the commissar: everything's in order."

With a crowbar over his shoulder and a shovel in his hand he made his way to the roof. Once there he selected a corner at the end opposite that where Katonin was at work.

A grey frozen pile towered in front of him consisting of a heterogeneous collection of rubbish. The leg of a broken chair stuck out like a bone from a meat jelly. He set to work slowly in order to get into the swing of the crowbar and at first his arms ached considerably. His strokes were irregular and he grew tired very quickly.

He decided to tackle the job from the top of the pile. With his crowbar he cut some steps, climbed up and began to shovel down the rubbish, snow and ice. He had been working for a couple of hours when his shovel hit against something hard and a head appeared from under the snow.

He squatted down in surprise and looked at the marble head as though it were a miracle. And indeed it was a most amazing spectacle: from this pile of frozen junk which defied all description peered the face, the beautiful face of a woman with her hair done up in a knot behind, a lovely and somewhat haughty face.

"Well, I declare!" he said wiping his forehead. "If I were to tell anyone—why nobody would believe me. Still, I'd better be getting on with the job."

But now, using the utmost caution, he cleared away the snow and broke up the ice and rubble in which the statue was buried. He made his way downstairs, dined, took part in a consultation, discussed matters with his col-

82

leagues, but strange to say—he caught himself thinking about that statue on the roof more often than it was worth. Day after day he showed up on the roof and when, on one occasion, one of the orderlies armed with a shovel offered to relieve him he brandished his crowbar at the man and shouted angrily:

"There's enough work, my good man, for everybody. Run along and give Doctor Katonin a hand. I'll manage here myself."

One day he climbed down from his ice hill and going up to Doctor Katonin tugged him cautiously by the sleeve:

"Yes, what is it, Ivan Nikolayevich?" he asked.

"I need your advice on a small...."

"But the consultation has been fixed for this evening...." Katonin began.

"It's not that, it's not that," Ivan Nikolayevich interrupted him, "I would like to have your advice at once. Come along, it's only two steps away, please...."

Katonin followed him along the roof and when he came to Ivan Nikolayevich's corner he saw a magnificent torso protruding from the dirty snow, gleaming strangely white against the background of charred wall.

"What do you make of it?" Ivan Nikolayevich asked. "Quite by chance, you know, I've become a bit of an archæologist here...."

In my opinion, Ivan Nikolayevich, it's a Venus," Katonin said with the look of a connoisseur, and he even took two paces back so as to take it in the better, shading his eyes with his hand.

"I think so too," Ivan Nikolayevich said. From what I've read up till now I always thought that Venus came from the sea, that she was born out of the surf, and here—God alone knows out of what. Still, she's being born and it is not Zeus who is creating her but an old surgeon, with a crowbar in his hand, and yet, nevertheless, he's creating her. Just watch—it won't take me long...."

"I must say you're doing a quick job," Katonin re-

6*

marked grudgingly. "It's true, of course, you have a Venus here. I haven't anything like that in my section of the roof."

That day Ivan Nikolayevich, a tired but satisfied look on his face, slowly made the round of the various floors where the work of renovation was proceeding apace. Everything attracted his attention. He stopped in one place to discuss the merits of a hole in the floor and advised two flushed nurses who had invented a mixture of some kind with which to fill the fissures in the floor to add some putty. He took a big brush out of the hands of an astounded nurse and set to painting the jambs, instructing her at the same time:

"That's not the way to do it. Now watch me—you've got to lay the paint on lightly, evenly. D'you see the difference? Your strokes are all awry. You've got to do it more evenly, more evenly."

Standing in the middle of a clean, newly painted ward, he remarked aloud:

"Not at all bad that blue touch. Whose idea was it?"

A young nurse with rosy cheeks replied in a cheerful voice:

"We had no other colour, comrade surgeon, so we had to use blue."

"I've nothing against it," he said. "On the contrary, it's splendid but what's most important, it's neat and clean. . . ."

In the evening, at supper, he said in the small room in which the doctors had their meals:

"It's really remarkable what an invigorating effect the spring has. It's a pleasure to stroll through the streets nowadays. The way the people have brightened up—they don't look so blue; and the children—they're so lively that if you're not careful they are sure to go dashing into you on their roller-skates. And the way the girls smile. . . . Even the ruined buildings do not look so repulsive as they did in the winter. And the air. . . . Only a short while ago, in one of the rooms which must have been an office —you know the one which has all sorts of fancy work on the ceiling—I saw an old woman ensconced right under that ceiling; a round table served as a basis, on top of that was a smaller table and on top of that was a step ladder; and there she was sitting astride that shaky construction cleaning the wood carving with a rag as if she'd done it all her life. A real acrobatic number...."

Day by day order grew in the house. It was evident that the job undertaken by the amateurs was a success. Small tables covered with a fresh coat of paint stood alongside the beds; the windows had been cleaned and polished until they shone; the baths were once more white and water flowed into the wash-basins; everybody was satisfied; people recalled how apprehensive they had been when first they saw the terrible state of the house which had been turned over to them.

Of late the surgeon had been suffering from insomnia. As a rule he used to be an early riser in the spring but now he could not get a wink of sleep. Lying awake until dawn he got up, dressed, washed, ate a crust of bread sprinkled with salt so as not to smoke on an empty stomach and rolling a cigarette made his way to the roof.

He sat down on the parapet, his legs dangling over just like a schoolboy. He looked at the Venus discovered by him, a rosy hue in the first rays of the morning sun. He had cleared away the last of the rubbish the evening before and now the statue, ensconced once again on its pedestal, stood there just as tranquilly as it had before that terrible winter which had spared neither humans nor the statue.

The vast city was bathed in a flaming sea of crystal light as though the agglomeration of buildings which stretched to the horizon were an enormous battery generating power. The city looked so young, so strong and there was such an air of spring about it that Ivan

Nikolayevich felt that he must be up and doing and, springing lightly from the parapet, he began to pace the roof, always coming back, however, to have a look at the statue. And it seemed to him that at any moment the statue would burst out laughing at his expense, at his absurd feelings, his awkwardness, his hurried steps at such an hour when people were still in their beds.

The morning was so glorious that he sat, walked, smoked and thought of life, of the city, of the war, of those whose lives he had saved on the blood-stained operating table, of the days he had spent cleaning up the filth, rubbish and snow with crowbar and shovel.

He came to a stop in front of the statue and said in a half whisper:

"You know how strong man can be. Nothing on earth is stronger than his free will, and how gifted—to build such a city, create such a statue—and along come these vandals and want to destroy it all. Damned if they do. Let them only try! We'll see who'll win through!"

"Admiring your handiwork?" came the familiar voice of the commissar behind him. "It's a magnificent statue. You haven't fallen in love with it, by chance, have you, doctor? Why are you up so early?"

The doctor paced the roof alongside the commissar. He felt ill at ease that the commissar had caught him preoccupied with his own thoughts and he parried the good-natured sorties.

"What is there to fall in love with here? The shoulder is crooked, the arm twisted. . . ."

"So you were studying it from a professional point of view, Ivan Nikolayevich?"

"Of course, from a professional point of view," Ivan Nikolayevich said and left the roof arm in arm with the commissar who was in high spirits because it was evident to him that he would be able to open the new hospital two weeks ahead of schedule.

His Sweetheart

O N THE days when Lyuba was on duty in the ward we were all in excellent spirits. Charming and glowing with life, she would fly into the ward in the morning in her soft slippers without a sound, a visible ray of sunshine. The frost would still be blazing in vivid cold flames on her cheeks; her laughing, guileless eyes sparkled and danced, and the legless major in the last bed would invariably exclaim:

" 'A maiden's cheeks are brighter than roses. . . .' What do you say, Lyubochka, are we to go on living?"

"Absolutely!" she would reply in a clear ringing voice, breathing on her frozen fingers.

Putting her hands behind her back she would press up against the big black stove, a slim white figure whose business-like seriousness was as delightful and touching as a child's. While she was warming her hands she would babble away at the rate of about a thousand words a minute about everything: about the morning war communique, about what happened with the damp firewood, about what was cooking in the kitchen for lunch, about the movies she had seen the day before. And little by little the moaning in the ward would quieten down, faces that testified to agonizing pain would clear up, the pallingly dreary hospital air of the ward freshened, sorrow grew lighter, and thoughts looked up and smiled.

Then she would place her slender fingers on her neck to see whether they had thawed out, her straight little nose would wrinkle up in a preoccupied way, she would throw a rapid, experienced glance around the ward deciding where to start—and the workday of the ward nurse would begin.

Everything she did was done quickly and tenderly— she would wash the patients' hair without spilling a drop of water on the pillow, write letters for those who were unable to do so, immediately notice if a patient took a turn for the worse and send for the doctor, fight tenaciously and passionately for the life of a wounded man when he was on the brink of death, comfort those who seemed to have lost all rest, and lull them into tranquil and healing sleep.

We were all fond of her and perhaps all of us were in love with her. But jealousy was not allowed into our ward. And if in a free moment Lyuba would sit down beside some one of us and play a game of "Old Maid," we all knew that on that day he must be feeling worse than the rest of us.

On this day I was by right the first candidate for "Old Maid." I had not slept at night, worried about matters that have nothing to do with this story, and in the morning I could only manage to grimace in the semblance of a smile in reply to her greeting. It was amazing how this young woman, little more than a girl, immediately sensed something wrong in another's soul. She had just glanced at me and yet when she had finished her round she unerringly walked over to my bed with a pack of cards in her hand.

But we did not have a game. Her child-like mouth drooped bitterly, her merry eyes were sad, and suddenly it seemed to me that she was years and years old. The cards lay idly, the ten of spades, symbol of sorrow, looming black on the white counterpane, and we began to talk softly and unreservedly.

Her husband, a captain in the Tank Corps and a man of great courage which had already won him a decoration, had been reported missing. For a whole month she had

88

been unable to trace him. For a long month this young woman had come flying in to us with her sunny smile, and all the time her soul was heavy within her and her heart ached, while at night she would cry softly to herself in the dormitory, trying not to wake her friends. Yesterday she had asked for the day off and had looked up an old friend of her husband's, someone high up in the Tank Corps. He had taken her hand and said:

"I won't deceive you, Lyuba. Pavel got stranded in enemy-occupied territory. The others broke through, but he didn't return." He squeezed her hand to keep her from crying. "Now, keep a stiff upper lip, Lyuba, he may turn up yet. You see, you must wait. Of course, it's a great art—waiting. I promise to tell you when there'll be no need to wait any longer."

I looked at her and tried to find in myself the strength of character which was in this young woman. In face of her grief I forgot my own, but I could not find in my clumsy, awkward and selfish male soul those words of comfort and hope which she so lavishly bestowed on us all.

The major in the last bed groaned. His tormenting illusion had begun: it seemed to him that the soles of his amputated feet were itching. Lyuba jumped up and rushed over to him. And once again her eyes were as they had been before. The hurt, her own hurt, gave way before that of another. And no one in the ward saw how great a burden of sorrow lay on her slim girlish shoulders.

Shortly after, I was transferred to another hospital for a time. A week later I returned to the familiar ward. Many of the old patients were no longer there, new wounded had arrived, and in the bed next to mine I saw a big motionless dummy made of bandages.

This was a tank man who had been severely burned on the chest and face. Everything that could possibly burn on a human face had been burned on him: the hair, eyebrows, eyelashes and the skin itself. From the white gauze the bulging dark lenses of huge goggles leered ominously. The glasses kept out the light, protecting the pupils of the eye, which had been saved by a miracle, and keeping them from coming in contact with the bandage.

Beneath them a slit for the mouth had been cleverly and skilfully left. From this slit came human speech, living speech, the only conveyor of his thoughts and sensations.

The tank man was fighting against harrowing and protracted pain. He suffered tortures when his dressings were changed, but he wanted to live. He wanted to live and to return to the firing line again. This will to live seethed in the tongue-tied, indistinct speech that came from his seared lips.

He loved to talk. In his dark and solitary world he thirsted for companionship. The words that issued from the motionless bundle of gauze were muffled and strange, but after I had learned to understand these wounded, broken words, I could make out the sounds of valour, hatred and victory, the din of battle and contact with death, heard dreams and hopes, confessions and beliefs— everything that a twenty-two-year old man who was fleeing from the spectre of solitude could possibly tell a friend. A friend—for by night we had become fast friends with that sudden strong friendship that comes in battle or in illness.

I woke up before dawn, when it was still quite dark. The ward was breathing heavily, and from time to time a groan cut through this alarming breathing of strong male bodies that had been broken in battle. And from the fact that no soundless white shadow glided rapidly towards this groan I knew that Lyuba was not on duty. Most likely the other nurse was on duty—Fenya, a plain wo· man, no longer young, who tired quickly, and frequently fell asleep on the chair in front of the stove at night. I got up to go out for a smoke and I heard the tank man asking for water. Fearing that I might hurt him, I wanted to wake the nurse.

"Don't," he said. "It doesn't matter...."

I carefully poured a few mouthfuls of water through a funnel into the opening in the bandage, and, of course, wet the gauze. Very much embarrassed, I apologized.

"It doesn't matter," he repeated, and laughed, if the soft gasps could be called laughing. "Only she knows how to do it.... As if you were actually drinking with your own lips...."

"Who is she?"

"My sweetheart."

And I heard an unusual tale of love.

He spoke of a woman whom he had not seen and could not see. He called her by an old Russian love word, *"dushenka"* (little darling). He had called her this on the very first day, sensing in her a special tenderness and warmth of heart, and he continued to call her this because his burnt lips would not let him say her name. "It's Lyuba, of course," I thought. Her name would indeed sound strange pronounced by him since his mutilated lips could not frame the letter "b": Lyuba—Lyusha....

He spoke of her with the utmost feeling, pride and, strange to say, passion. Dreaming out loud, he pictured her to himself, describing her face, her eyes, her smile, and I was amazed by this second sight of love which had indeed descried the beloved image. Lowering his voice he confessed that he knew her hair, the fine silky hair that tumbled from under her cap: once he had touched it when he had tried with his blind fingers to help her find the thermometer case, which had fallen behind the night table. He spoke of her hands—tender, strong, careful hands, which he held in his for hours, telling her about himself, about his childhood, about the fighting, about the tank explosion, about his solitude and the horrible life of a cripple which awaited him.

He told me everything that she had said to comfort

him, all her tender words of hope, her faith that he would be able to see, to live and fight again, and it seemed to me that I could hear the voice of Lyuba herself. In an almost inaudible whisper he told me that tomorrow was the deciding day: the professor had promised to remove his goggles and perhaps he would begin to see. He had not told this to "Dushenka"—what if he would not be able to see? Better that she should not suffer. If it would come to nothing, it would come to nothing—in any case he knew her face. It was beautiful and sweet and in her eyes he could see love. Then there was something else: she had talked him into a delicate operation which would return to him his eyebrows, eyelashes and fresh pink skin. He knew at what price of pain he would buy this new face for himself, but he was willing to go through anything for the sake of his sweetheart.

Yes, his sweetheart. He repeated this word with pride. Her husband had fallen at the front not so long ago. She was alone, just as he was, and even more unfortunate than he: he had lost only his face, while she had lost a beloved person. In the course of the long nights they had learned all there was to know about one another, and love had come to this ward where death stalked. Life, brought by love, gained the upper hand over him. For there had been a time when he had wanted to shoot himself—what was the sense of his continuing to live a cripple? . . . Now everything was different. He was living in hopes of the future, fighting for life, for health, for strength, for happiness, for the chance to take revenge on the enemy for himself and for others.

"She told me that it doesn't matter what the result will be with my face. She said to me, I love you and not your face, you see. . . ."

And he wept. I could tell that he was crying because his breast, filled with happiness, heaved and his breath became laboured.

Leaving him to himself, I lay down quietly in my own

bed, thinking about Lyuba. I wondered at her strange fate. Was this real love, the inexplicable love of a noble woman's soul, or tender pity, which is so often akin to love? Or perhaps it was the sharing of a sorrow, the horror of a loss, the finding of the ghost of what she had lost: a tank man, a hero, a fighter.... I waited impatiently for morning and the shift of the nurses in order to read Lyuba at a glance and see the answer—in such eyes everything was plain to see. With these thoughts I fell asleep.

I woke up late. By the familiar signs of the ward day I realized that the nurses had already shifted, but Lyuba was not in the ward. I walked over to the tank man and asked him how he felt.

"Fine," he replied. "She's gone to find out about my dressing. Only listen here, not a word about the professor. Will I really be able to see today?"

By his voice I could guess that he was smiling.

"She's a real beauty; you know her, don't you?"

"That's true enough, she is beautiful," I replied.

Again he began to speak to me about how he would see her today. Suddenly he fell silent, and in silence listened to the steps, the light steps in felt slippers, and it was strange that through the bandages which muffled his head he was able to distinguish them. Or was it the ears of love that heard?

"It's she," he said softly. "My Dushenka...."

I turned around. But it was Fenya who came up. Evidently she had been detained after her shift. I wanted to tell him that he had made a mistake.

"Good morning, Fenichka," I said. "Will Lyuba be through soon?"

"Good morning. Back with us again?" she asked. "Lyuba's gone, she found her husband. He's wounded."

And she sat down beside the tank man.

"Kolya, dear," she said, caressingly. "Be strong.... We have to change your dressing now...."

93

He held out a trembling hand, and immediately this hand of a fighter, which had seen death and which was trembling in anticipation of the pain, found Fenya's hand. Evidently the dressing of his wounds was agonizing.

She covered it with her other hand, and a long and expressive silence fell over them. Softly she smoothed his hand and twined her fingers in his. And in her eyes, which were fixed on the dark glasses, there glowed the warm, slow fire of love.

I looked at her face—the undistinguished face which we had been seeing every day and which we had passed over with an indifferent glance. The amazing change in it astonished me. Elderly, tired, inspired by the force of love it was beautiful, the simple face of a Russian woman and mother filled with hope and sad tenderness. Then the tears welled up in her eyes and she softly turned her head aside so that they would not drop on his hand. But feeling this light movement he became alarmed.

"Dushenka, dear, what's the matter?"

And—astonishing thing—Fenya began to talk vivaciously and merrily, cheering him up while the tears coursed down her cheeks rapidly and without stop, and the deep hurt twisted her mouth from which these jolly and joking words came. Then her eyes turned to the door, and hopeless silent misery filled them. I followed her glance. a wheelcot was standing in the doorway, and I understood her tears. She was anticipating the approaching pain.

They put the tank man in the cot and Fenya walked beside him, holding his hand. I accompanied them. At the door of the bandaging room she left him. Her strength deserted her and leaning her head against the door jamb, she let her tears flow freely. I touched her on the shoulder. She raised her eyes.

"The professor told me. . . . The professor told me. . . ."

She was unable to speak.

"I know," I replied. "But why do you upset yourself ahead of time. . . . Of course, he will see."

She shook her head as if with pain.

"And he will see me.... Where do I compare to what he imagines.... What has he invented about me, why has he invented these things?... Beautiful, beautiful.... Oh, leave me alone!" she suddenly exclaimed, almost shouting, and pressed her ear to the door.

I could hear the professor's cheerful voice through the door: "That's enough, that'll do for the first time. Just one more week in the dark!"

Fenya grew pale with the terrible pallor of despair and quickly walked down the corridor.

No one ever saw her in the hospital any more. Later we found out that she had gone back to her home town—a woman with a great soul who preferred to go away in order to leave with the man whom she had returned to life and victory a beautiful dream about a beautiful young woman who loved him for himself alone and not his face, rather than disclose to him the truth which would shatter his dreams.

VADIM KOZHEVNIKOV

Captain Zhavoronkov

H IS FLYING togs torn to tatters, with holes in them burned through in places while he dozed of a night by a campfire, hung loosely on his emaciated body. His red, unkempt beard and the deep lines on his face ingrained with dirt, made him look much older than he was.

Captain Pyotr Zhavoronkov had baled out behind the enemy's lines in March on a special mission and now, what with the thaw setting in and rivulets and streams swelling up everywhere, it was no easy matter trying to make his way back through the woods in his soddened felt boots. At first he had travelled only by night. During the day he had hidden away in some hole or other. But now, afraid that hunger would completely undermine his strength, he was pushing on in the daytime too.

The Captain had carried out his mission. The only thing that remained to be done was to locate the radio operator who had been dropped somewhere in the vicinity some two months ago.

"Carried out his mission!" How simple it sounded now. How much vital weight and physical energy he had lost on this job—he who had never had an ounce of superfluous weight.

During the last four days he had had next to nothing to eat. Pressing on through the sodden forest his famished eyes lingered longingly on the white trunks of the birch trees the bark of which—he knew—could be pounded to

96

dust and cooked in the tin where he had carried his supply of T.N.T. and eaten—a bitterish sort of gruel, true, with a woody flavour.

When things went hard with him the Captain had a way of arguing with himself as though he had a worthy and staunch companion at his side.

"Now bearing in mind the extraordinary circumstances," the Captain ruminated, "you can make your way to the nearest highway. In that case, by the way, you'll have a chance of getting a change of footwear. But, generally speaking, to make a raid on solitary German transports is a sign that you're almost at the end of your tether. And, as the saying goes, the clamouring of your stomach is drowning the voice of reason."

Accustomed to being alone for long periods at a stretch, the Captain could go on arguing with himself until he either grew weary or, as he admitted to himself, he began to talk nonsense.

It seemed to him that this other, second fellow with whom he argued, was not at all a bad sort of a chap, one you could talk to, whose heart was in the right place and sympathetic. Only on rare occasions did the Captain cut him short roughly: "Hey, you, you can gas as much as you like but don't forget to keep your eyes peeled." He would pull himself up this way at the slightest rustle or when he caught sight of ski tracks in the melting snow.

The Captain's opinion about his double being a fellow after one's heart, one who understood things, differed somewhat from the opinions of his comrades. In the squadron the Captain was regarded as being a far from congenial person. Laconic, reserved, he did not imbue others with a desire for friendly confidences. He never found a friendly cheering word for newcomers who were going out on a job for the first time; on the contrary, in a most subtle manner he would do his utmost to scare them with the dangers in store for them; then he would really wax eloquent.

Sometimes he would turn a man out of the plane just before it took off.

"Coward," he would shout. "I don't need the likes of you!" And he would slam the trap door to.

Returning after some successful job the Captain would do his utmost to evade the congratulations of the men, slipping away on the flimsiest of excuses:

"Pardon me, fellows, I simply must have a shave, I look more like a hedgehog just now," and off he would go to his own quarters.

He was never fond of talking about his work in the rear of the Germans and confined himself to reporting to his superior officer. Resting after a job he would loll about on his bed and turn up for dinner with a drowsy and sullen look on his face.

"Not a very interesting chap," was the general opinion. "Rather a bore."

At one time a rumour went round which served to justify his conduct. It was said that his family had been killed off by the Germans at the very beginning of the war. Hearing the rumour the Captain turned up to dinner one day holding a letter in his hand. He kept it in front of him all the time he was eating his soup.

"From my wife," he remarked offhandedly.

The men exchanged glances. Many of them with a look of chagrin—for they wanted to believe that the Captain was such a recluse because of some great sorrow. But it turned out quite the reverse.

Then again, the Captain simply detested the violin. The sound of a violin reacted on him like the scraping of a knife on glass does on others.

The forest was bare and dripping. The soggy ground was full of holes, filled with dirty water—last year's snow turning into slush. It was a miserable job to tramp through such a bleak place, alone, dead beat.

The Captain, however, had deliberately chosen this bleak route. There would be less probability of meeting

Germans on the way. And the more dismal and dreary the place looked the more confidently did he press forward.

The only drawback was the pangs of hunger which were making themselves felt so. At times a mist rose before his eyes. He stopped and rubbed his eyes and when that did not help he punched his face with his fist in order to send the blood to his head.

Making his way down a gully the Captain turned towards a tiny waterfall which trickled over a cliff rimmed with ice and began to drink. The taste of the snow water produced a feeling of nausea. But he went on drinking nevertheless in order to stop the gnawing at the pit of his stomach.

Evening came. Faint shadows lay on the thin, slushy snow. It grew cold. The puddles froze over and the ice crackled under foot. The wet branches became coated with ice; when he pushed them aside with his hand they tinkled like glass. However much the Captain tried to make his way silently, every step of his was accompanied by a cracking and snapping.

The moon came up. The forest was aglow. Innumerable icicles and icy puddles reflecting the light of the moon sparkled like Bengal lights.

The radio operator must be somewhere in the vicinity. But how could he expect to find him at once if the spot in question covered an area of about four kilometres? The man, probably, had found himself a retreat hidden away no less snugly than the lair of a wild beast.

After all he couldn't go shouting through the woods: "Hey, comrade! Where are you?"

The Captain made his way through a grove flooded with moonlight. His felt boots frozen by the night frost became heavy and stiff, like clogs.

He was vexed at the radio operator because it was so difficult to find the man. But he would have been angrier still had he found him without any difficulty.

7*

Stumbling over the trunk of a tree buried under an old snowdrift the Captain went sprawling on the ground. And when with difficulty he got onto his knees, steadying himself with his hands in the snow, he heard the metallic click of a revolver being cocked behind his back.

"Halt!" came a whispered order. "Halt!"

The Captain behaved rather queerly. Without turning round he began to rub his injured knee. But when in the same whisper he was ordered in German to put his hands up the Captain turned round and said scoffingly:

"When a chap's down already, what's the use of crying 'Halt!'? You should have gone for me at once and plugged me with that revolver of yours, wrapping it up in your cap—then the shot would be muffled and almost inaudible. And then again when a German challenges anybody he usually yells out 'Halt' at the top of his voice so that his neighbour should also hear him and, in case of necessity, come to his aid. Here we are teaching you and teaching you and all to no purpose...." The Captain scrambled to his feet. He gave the password in a whisper that could barely be heard. When he was given the counter-sign he nodded his head and, adjusting the safety cap, slipped his revolver back into his pocket.

"But yet you kept your gun ready!"

The Captain glared angrily at the radio operator.

"You didn't expect me to depend only on your being a wise guy, did you? Look here," he demanded impatiently, "better show me where that den of yours is!"

"After me," the radio operator said remaining on his knees in an unnatural posture, "I'll crawl along."

"There's no need to crawl, there's nobody about in these woods."

"My foot's frozen," the radio operator explained in a whisper. "It hurts awfully."

The Captain snorted and followed the man who was crawling along on all fours.

"What fool tricks have you been up to, running around barefoot, eh?"

"The plane was rocking like the dickens when I baled out. One of my felt boots slipped off when I was still in the air."

"You're a nice one." And then he added: "It'll be a fine job getting out of here with you."

The radio operator sat down supporting himself on his hands in the snow.

"Now look here, Comrade Captain," he said, a tone of resentment in his voice, "I don't intend to leave. You can leave me some food and clear off. When my foot's better, I'll manage myself."

"Oh, yes? You can just see me rigging up a sanatorium for you! The Germans didn't get your bearings by any chance?" Bending down suddenly the Captain asked in alarm: "Hey, I say, what's your name? Your face seems familiar to me."

"Mikhailova."

"Plucky of you!" the Captain muttered. It was impossible to make out which predominated in his voice—embarrassment or resentment. "Oh, very well. Never mind. We'll get out of here somehow." Then he enquired politely: "Can I do anything to help you?"

The girl made no reply. She crawled on up to her elbows in the snow.

The Captain's feeling of exasperation gave way to something else, something less defined but more disturbing. He remembered this very same Mikhailova at his camp base where she went through a course of training. From the very first moment he clapped his eyes on her she went against the grain—even aroused bitter resentment in him. He simply could not make out why she was at the camp base—tall, beautiful, yes, very beautiful, with a proud tilt to her head and rich, finely moulded lips which seemed to hypnotize one when she spoke.

She had an unpleasant way of looking a person

straight in the eyes, unpleasant not because her eyes were repugnant; on the contrary, she had large, intelligent and steady eyes with a glint of gold around large pupils. Yes, she had splendid eyes. What he did not like about them was that they looked at one so intently that the Captain could not stand it. And the girl had noticed this.

And then again that manner of hers of doing her hair, fluffy, sparkling and golden which reached to the collar of her greatcoat!

How many times had the Captain told her:

"Tuck those pigtails of yours out of sight. A military uniform is not for a fancy-dress ball."

Mikhailova, it is true, was very persevering at her lessons: remaining behind after classes she often asked the Captain questions which revealed a good grasp of the subject. Convinced, however, that the knowledge would be of no use to her he replied briefly, tersely, looking impatiently at his watch all the time.

The superintendent of the courses admonished the Captain for giving such little attention to Mikhailova.

"She's a good girl."

"She's good enough for family life," and the Captain suddenly burst out passionately, heatedly: "Please understand, Comrade Superintendent, people in our particular line aren't allowed to have any ties. Circumstances may dictate our having to do away with ourselves, with our own hands. And she? Would she be able to do it? She'd be sorry for herself! What's the use of such like...."

To get rid of Mikhailova he transferred her to the radio operators' group.

The base camp where the scouts were undergoing training was located in one of the rest homes near Moscow. The wide, closed in verandas, the red-carpeted floors, the exquisite furniture—the whole atmosphere in general so reminiscent of the days of peace, inclined one to take things easy of an evening. Somebody would sit down at the piano and then they would have dances. And had it not been for the fact that everybody present was in military uniform, one might almost have believed that this was a usual week-end gathering in one of the many rest homes outside Moscow.

Anti-aircraft guns barked out, the white beams of the searchlights scoured the skies with their long tentacles—but one need not think of that.

Classes over, Mikhailova would often find herself a comfortable corner on a settee in the drawing-room deep in a book. She read by the light of a lamp with an enormous shade attached to a big, massive, mahogany stand. This girl with the beautiful, tranquil face, restful pose, hair loose down her back, and fingers so slender and white, somehow did not fit in with the technique of a sapper, to wield a knife the shaft of which was made of rubber so as to give one a better grip.

When Mikhailova caught sight of the Captain she would jump up and draw herself up to attention as the regulations required when an officer appeared.

Captain Zhavoronkov would walk past giving her a careless nod. Again that feeling of exasperation would rise up in him.

This strong man with the tanned, gaunt face of a sportsman, somewhat tired and sad, it is true, was hard and exacting even to himself.

... German sappers had mined the country lanes which fed the trunk road. At night he shot the man on point duty with a small-calibre pistol which fired almost soundlessly and, armed with the man's lantern, took his place on the road.

He regulated the traffic, giving the required signals—green or red. When a tank column appeared he switched on the red light barring its way along the main road and gave the green light directing it to one of the mined country lanes.

... Stumbling across a telephone line connecting the

German staff headquarters he cut the wire and lay in wait. A signaller showed up. He was accompanied by several automatic riflemen. Having repaired the line the signaller went off. The Captain ripped the insulating tape from the wire and placed it on the ground. His ruse worked just as he had planned. Ascertaining that the line was not working properly the signaller returned, but alone this time. The Captain stabbed him through. Coiling up the line he threw it into a hayrick and set fire to it.

On another occasion he crawled onto the roof of a German bunker and dropped the contents of his cartridge case down the chimney. He shot down the Germans who came tumbling out from under cover with his automatic rifle.

The Captain preferred to do a lone job. He had every right. His heart had become chilled with an icy pain ever since the death of his wife and child. They had been mangled to death on the very first day of the war under the treads of a column of tanks that swept through the frontier settlement where they lived.

The Captain did not care to show his grief. He did not want people to imagine that this sorrow of his was the cause of his daring. That was why he tried to deceive his comrades. He said to himself: "My wife and my child have not been killed, they're alive. I'm not petty. I'm like everybody else. I must fight cold-bloodedly." No, he was not petty. He concentrated all his efforts on the exacting of vengeance. During this war one meets with many such men, men with wounded hearts, proud men, sorrowful and strong.

Good, happy, kind people! What must you have suffered to have hardened your hearts so! And now, walking behind the radio operator who crawled on in front, the Captain tried not to think of anything that would hinder him from drawing up a plan of action. He was hungry, weak, exhausted by his long journey and the pain from his frozen foot. She, of course, was reckoning on his help. But, then, she did not know that he wasn't fit for anything.

Tell her how things were? No, nothing doing! Better make her buck up somehow and in the meantime he'd husband his strength and then, maybe, he'd be able to manage somehow....

On the steep slope of a hill the turbulent spring waters had washed away something in the nature of a cave. The powerful intertwining tree roots hung overhead, some thin like cord, others twisted and wiry, resembling more a bundle of rusty hawsers. A roof of ice hid the cave from sight. In the daytime the light penetrated into the cave as through a glassed veranda. Inside it was clean and dry, the floor covered with a layer of pine branches. The only fittings were a square box containing the radio apparatus, a sleeping bag and a pair of skis leaning against the wall.

"Quite a snug place," the Captain remarked. And touching the matting on the floor he said: "Here, sit down and take your thing off."

"What!" the girl exclaimed indignantly, in surprise.

"Take your things off. I've got to know what you're good for with that game leg of yours."

"You're not a doctor. And then again...."

"Look here," the Captain said, "we'd better come to an understanding from the very start—less back talk."

"Oh, that hurts!"

"Stop squealing," the Captain said running his hand over her foot which was all black and blue and swollen.

"That'll do, it's unbearable."

"Well, you've got to stick it," the Captain said. He took off the woollen scarf he had around his neck.

"I don't want your scarf."

"You prefer that stinking stocking of yours?"

"It doesn't stink, it's clean."

"Look here," the Captain repeated, "don't try and kid me. Have you a bit of string?"

"No."

The Captain raised his hand, tore off a length of thin root and bound the foot wrapped up in his scarf.

"Now it'll hold," he declared.

After that he took the skis outside and got busy with a knife the shaft of which was made of rubber. He came back, took the radio apparatus and said:

"Come on, let's be going."

"You want to lug me along on those skis?"

"I don't want to, as a matter of fact, it's a case of having to."

"Just as you like—I have no choice in the matter."

"Now, that's the right spirit," the Captain agreed. "By the way, you haven't anything to eat, have you?" he asked.

"Here," she said, taking a bit of broken biscuit out of her pocket.

"Doesn't look much."

"It's all I have left. For several days already...."

"Everything's clear," the Captain said. "Others usually eat their biscuits first and leave the chocolate for a rainy day."

"You can keep your chocolate to yourself."

"I don't in the least intend to treat you,"—and the Captain left the cave bending double under the weight of the heavy radio apparatus.

After plodding on for an hour the Captain realized that he was on his last legs. And although the girl lying on the skis, or rather the sled made out of the skis, helped him as best as she could by trundling the thing along with her arms, he felt his strength giving out. His legs were shaky and his heart was pounding in a way that it seemed to stick in his throat.

"If I tell her I'm absolutely done in, she'll get panicky. But if I go on braving it out things will end pretty rotten," he thought to himself.

The Captain looked at his watch.

"It wouldn't be a bad thing," he said, "to drink something hot."

"Have you any vodka?"

"Vodka!" the Captain exclaimed. "You needn't budge, all the same I won't give you any vodka."

Digging a hole in the snow he made a flueway with a stick and covered the exit with some green branches and snow. The branches and the snow would serve as a filter for the smoke and then it would not be noticeable. Gathering some dry twigs, the Captain put them into the hole and then, taking from his pocket a small silk bag in which he kept some powder, he sprinkled a handful onto the twigs and put a match to it.

The flames began to rise, licking the branches. He placed his T.N.T. tin on the fire and filled it up with bits of ice. After that he took the broken biscuit, wrapped it up in his handkerchief and, putting it on the stump of a tree, pounded it into a powder with the handle of his knife. This he put into the boiling water and began to stir it. Taking the tin off the fire he set it down on the snow to cool off.

"Is it nice?" the girl asked.

"Almost like coffee," the Captain replied, handing her the tin with the brown concoction.

"No, thanks, I can go without," the girl said.

"You'll have to go without a lot before I've finished with you," the Captain said. "But, in the meantime, stop playing the fool. Here, drink this."

Towards evening he managed to kill an old rook with a stick.

"Are you really going to eat that crow?" she asked.

"It's not a crow but a rook," the Captain replied.

He grilled the bird over the campfire.

"D'you want any?"—he offered her half.

"Not for anything!" she replied turning away in disgust.

The Captain hesitated for a moment and then he said thoughtfully:

"Yes, it will only be fair,"—and he ate the whole bird himself.

Lighting a cigarette he felt more cheerful and asked: "How's your foot?"

"I think I could manage to walk a bit," the girl replied.

"Forget about it!"

All night long the Captain dragged the sled while the girl dozed fitfully.

Towards daybreak he stopped in a gully.

An enormous pine—torn up by the roots during a storm—lay on the ground. Under the mighty roots was a hollow. The Captain cleared away the snow, strewed the bottom with some branches and spread a shelter tent over them.

"You want to sleep?" the girl asked, waking up.

"For an hour, not more," the Captain said. "I've almost forgotten how to sleep by now."

The girl began to scramble out of her sleeping bag.

"Hey, what are you up to?" the Captain asked, raising himself on his elbow.

The girl went up to him and said:

"I'm going to turn in with you. It'll be warmer that way. We'll cover ourselves with the bag."

"Well, I'm...." the Captain began.

"Move over," the girl said. "After all you don't want me to lie in the snow, do you? ... Are you uncomfortable?"

"Take your hair away, its tickling my nose. I feel like sneezing, and in general...."

"I thought you wanted to sleep! Well, go to sleep. My hair won't interfere with you."

"But it does," the Captain mumbled drowsily and fell sound asleep.

The only noise was the dripping of the melting snow.

Scurrying clouds, like whisks of smoke, threw fleeting shadows on the snow.

The Captain slept, his fist to his lips, a tired and exhausted look on his face. The girl bent over him and cautiously slipped her arm under his head.

Heavy drops of water dripped from the canopy of branches over the hollow. The girl took her arm away and shielded the face of the sleeping man with her palm. When it became filled with water she just as carefully poured it out.

The Captain opened his eyes, sat up and began to rub his face with the palms of his hands.

"Your hair's grey at the temples," the girl remarked. "Is it the result of that incident?"

"Which one?" the Captain asked, stretching himself.

"The time when you were sentenced to be shot."

"I don't remember," the Captain said with a yawn. He did not feel inclined to remember that incident.

It happened as follows. In August the Captain blew up a large German ammunition dump. He suffered from shellshock as a result of the air blast and was scorched by the flames. When the German ambulance men picked him up he was lying on the ground in his charred and still smoldering clothes. Together with the other German soldiers who had suffered he was sent to a hospital. He was laid up for three weeks. Before being sent to the rear the wounded men were interrogated by a special commission. The Captain, together with a group of men who were feigning sickness, was sentenced to be shot. They were reprieved at the very last minute. Instead, they were bundled onto a transport plane and sent somewhere in the vicinity of Yelna. Here they were forced to launch a "psychological" attack against the Russians, a company of automatic riflemen behind them to spur them on. The Captain was wounded by a bullet from our own men. He was picked up and the next two weeks he spent in one of our hospitals.

In order to change the subject the Captain asked somewhat roughly but insistently:

"Does your foot still hurt?"

"I've told you already that I can walk," she replied irritably.

"Good. Now get on the sled. When the time comes you'll hop along yet."

The Captain harnessed himself to the makeshift sled and again he plodded on through the slush.

It was raining and snowing at the same time. The ground was slippery. Every now and then he would step into a hole filled with slush. It was a grey and dreary day. And just as drearily the Captain wondered whether they would manage to cross the ice of the river which was most probably already covered with water.

A dead horse lay across their path.

The Captain squatted down over it and took out his knife with the rubber shaft.

"You know," the girl said getting up from the sled, "you do everything so efficiently that it's a pleasure to watch you."

"You're simply hungry, that's all," the Captain replied laconically.

He roasted several thin slices of meat using the antenna in place of a spit.

"It's tasty!" the girl said in surprise.

"Of course," the Captain replied, "roasted horsemeat is much better than beef."

After his meal he got up and said:

"I'll go along and reconnoitre the ground. You stay here."

"Very well," she agreed. "You may think me silly but I'm beginning to find it very hard to be left alone now. I've somehow become accustomed to being together."

"Now look here! None of that nonsense!" the Captain replied.

110

But this applied more to himself because he felt confused.

He came back after dark.

The girl was sitting on the sled, her revolver in her lap. When she caught sight of him she smiled and got up.

"Sit down, sit down," the Captain said in the tone he had been accustomed to use in class. He rolled himself a cigarette and looking at the girl as though sizing her up, he said:

"I've spotted something worth while. The Germans have rigged up an aerodrome not far from here."

"So what?" the girl asked.

"Oh, nothing," the Captain replied. "They've done it so cutely." Then he asked her seriously: "Is your apparatus in working order?"

"You want to get in touch?" the girl asked brightening up.

"Yes," the Captain said.

Mikhailova took off her cap and adjusted the headphones. Several minutes later she asked the Captain what he would like to transmit. The Captain sat down beside her. Bringing his fist down on the palm of his hand he said:

"In short it's like this: my map's spoilt from being in the water. I can't indicate the exact location of the aerodrome. I'm giving the coordinates according to the compass. Owing to the low ceiling all ground bearings will be covered from sight. Our radio on wave length... give your wave length... will serve as their guide to the spot."

The girl took off her headphones. Her face beamed happily as she turned towards the Captain.

The Captain, however, rolling a new cigarette, did not even glance at her.

"Now look here," he said dully. "I'm going to take that radio apparatus of yours and go over there," he indicated the direction with his hand and explained: "In order to be nearer to the target. You'll have to make your way back as best as you can. As soon as it gets dark slip down to the river. The ice is very thin so take a pole or something suitable with you. If the ice gives under you it'll come in handy. Once you're across make for Malinovka. It's about three kilometres away. Somebody'll meet you there."

"That's all very well," Mikhailova said, "only I'm afraid I can't give you the apparatus."

"Here, none of that," the Captain said.

"I'm responsible for the apparatus and I'm going to stick to it."

"As a sort of free supplement," the Captain blurted out. Flaring up he said loudly: "I order you."

"You know, Captain, that every one of your orders will be carried out. But, you know very well that you have no right to take the apparatus away from me."

"But do try and understand," the Captain said in a furious temper.

"I do understand," Mikhailova replied calmly. "What you intend to do is my job." And looking the Captain angrily in the eyes she said: "Here you go boiling over and want to tackle a job that's actually none of your business."

The Captain turned away abruptly. He wanted to say something, something that would offend her, something that would make her smart but checking himself he said with an effort:

"All right, go ahead, you do it." And as though to get his own back he said: "Of course, you couldn't think of it yourself and now...."

Mikhailova looked at him scoffingly.

"I thank you very much for the idea," she said.

The Captain looked at his watch.

"What are you sitting here for? Time's short."

Mikhailova picked up the apparatus by the shoulder

112

straps, took several paces and then glanced round towards the Captain.

"Goodbye, Captain," she said.

"Go on, go on," he blurted out and turned away in the direction of the river.

A slight mist covered the ground, the air reeked of dampness and everywhere could be heard the murmuring of running water which did not freeze even at night. To die in such weather was particularly unpleasant. As a matter of fact it was not very pleasant to die in any weather.

Had Mikhailova, say, some three months ago, read a novel in which the heroine had gone through adventures that had fallen to her lot, a dreamy look would have undoubtedly come into her beautiful eyes; drawing herself up cosily under her soft quilts she would have pictured herself in place of the heroine; at the end only, in revenge for all she had suffered, she would have saved the life of the haughty hero. And then he would fall in love with her but she would not pay the slightest attention to him.

That evening when she told her father what she had decided on she did not know that the work would demand such a super-human effort, that she would have to learn to sleep in the mud, go hungry, freeze in the open, be lonely and miserable. But had anybody told her in detail what was in store for her, how hard it would be, she would have asked simply:

"But other people can do it?"

"Suppose you're killed?"

"Not everybody's killed."

"And if they torture you?"

She would have pondered for a while and then said as though to herself:

"I don't know. I can't say how I'd behave. What I do know is that I won't say anything. And you know that too."

And when her father heard that her mind was made up his head dropped onto his chest and he said in a hoarse voice she could hardly recognize:

"It'll be hard, very hard now for your mother and me."

"Papa," she said appealingly, "Papa, but do try and understand. I simply can't stay at home."

Her father lifted his face and she was aghast—how old and weary he looked.

"I do understand," her father said. "Well, it would have been worse had my daughter been different."

"Papa!" she exclaimed, "Papa, you're so good to me that I'm almost ready to cry."

She had told her mother the next morning that she was joining some military courses as a telephone operator.

Her mother had turned pale but trying not to show her emotion she had said:

"Only take care of yourself, darling."

During the course of training Mikhailova had studied diligently and during the exams had been as excited as when she had taken her exams at school; and how happy she had been when she learned that she had received excellent marks. The Captain, however, was right. Alone in the woods during those terrible, cold, black nights, she had given way at first to tears and consoled herself by eating up all the chocolate. She had transmitted at regular intervals, and although at times she had terribly wanted to add something, something of her own so as to dispel that feeling of loneliness, she had refrained from doing so, so as not to use up the battery.

And now, making her way to the aerodrome, she was surprised how simple it had been. Here she was crawling through the slush, wet to the skin, her foot frozen. When in the old days she was laid up with the grippe her father would sit at her bedside and read aloud to her so that she should not strain her eyes. And her mother, with a look of concern on her face, would warm the thermometer in her hands because her daughter did not like to measure her temperature with a cold thermometer. And when somebody rang up her mother would whisper in distress: "Yes, she's sick." And her father would muffle the telepehone so that when it rang the bell would not disturb his daughter. And now, if the Germans were quick in detecting the bearings of her radio, she would be killed for sure.

Yes, they would kill her, she who was so nice, so beautiful and good and, perhaps, gifted. And they would leave her lying in that hateful, wet snow. And she was in fur-lined flying togs. The Germans, most likely, would strip her. And she shuddered, picturing herself lying naked in the mud. And the soldiers, with abominable looks in their eves, would stare at her, at her naked body.

This forest so resembled that grove at Kratovo where she had spent one summer. There were the same kind of trees there. And when she was in the Pioneers' Camp there were the same kind of trees there too. And there was a hammock there, tied to two twin trees just like those over there.

And when that time Dimka carved her name on the bark of a birch tree—just like that one over there—she had been angry because he had injured the tree and she would not speak to him. And he had followed her and looked at her with sad and, therefore, beautiful eyes. And later on, when they had made it up, he had told her that he wanted to kiss her. She had closed her eyes and said pathetically: "Only not on the lips." And he was so excited that he kissed her on the chin.

She was very fond of beautiful clothes. On one occasion when she was sent to make a report somewhere she had put on her best dress. Her friends had asked: "Why the glad rags?"

Looking at herself in the mirror she had thought to herself: "I'm happy. It's so nice to be beautiful."

And now she was crawling over the ground, dirty, wet, her eyes taking in everything, her ears intent, dragging her frozen, swollen foot after her.

"So they'll kill me. So what? After all, Dimka was killed and others too—such splendid chaps. Well, and I'll be killed. Am I any better than they?"

It was snowing. The puddles squelched under her. Old snow lay in patches in the hollows. She crawled on and on. Stopping to rest she would lie flat on the wet ground her head on the hollow of her arm. She had no strength to crawl to a dry spot.

And again she crawled on with the doggedness of a wounded man who crawls to a first aid station where his wound will be dressed, where he will get a drink of water, where he will find blissful rest and other people will look after him.

The mist grew black because the night, too, was black. And somewhere, above the clouds, enormous ships were winging on their way. The navigator of the flagship sitting in his chair, his eyes half-closed, listened intently to the slightest sound coming from the megaphones—but he could not catch the signals of the radio operator.

The pilots sitting in the cockpits, the radio operators and gunners in their places, also listened intently to the wheezing and screeching of the megaphones—but no signal was forthcoming. The propellers cleaved a way through the murky sky. The planes flew ever forward but still there was no signal.

And suddenly, hardly audible, came the first cautious signal. The enormous ships turned, steering their course by this flimsy thread of sound; ominous and heavy they ploughed through the cloud banks. The sound so dear, like the song of a cricket, like the rustling of the wheat or the dry autumn leaves in the breeze, served to guide the enormous steel ships.

The commander of the flight, the pilots, the radio operators and gunners, the flight mechanics—and Mikhailova too—knew: the bombs would go hurtling down to the spot where the radio transmitting the signal—a signal so dear, a call to arms—was located, because that was where the enemy planes were.

Mikhailova, on her knees in a pit filled with black, slimy water, bent over her apparatus, her hand working the key transmitting the signal. The sombre sky hung low over her head. It was empty and silent.

Her frozen foot became numb, her back ached and her temples too, as though somebody was squeezing her head with hot iron bands. She was feverish. When she put her hand to her lips it was hot and dry. "I've evidently caught a cold," she thought to herself moodily. "What does it matter now, anyway."

At times she felt that she was losing consciousness. She opened her eyes and listened fearfully. In the headphones she could hear the signal loudly and distinctly. Her hand, evidently, was automatically pressing the key transmitting the signal. "That's the result of training! It's a good thing I went and not the Captain. Could his hand work the signal automatically? But if I hadn't, I would have been in Malinovka by now and, maybe, somebody would have lent me a warm jacket...and there's a fire in the stove there... and everything would have been different. And soon nothing more will ever happen.... How strange things are. Here am I lying on the ground and thinking. But, somewhere, there's Moscow. And there are people there lots of people. And nobody knows I'm here. After all I am splendid! I wonder whether I'm brave? I don't seem to be a bit afraid. It's probably because I'm so sick—that's why I'm not afraid.... If only it would soon be all over. Really, what are they up to? Can't they realize that I simply can't stick it any longer?"

Dashing away a tear she lay down on her side on the slope of the pit and went on transmitting the signal. Now she could see the vast expanse of sombre sky. Suddenly, searchlights began to play on it and she could hear the distant heavy throbbing of the engines. And Mikhailova, swallowing her tears, whispered to herself:

"Oh you dears, you darlings. At last you've come for me. I'm feeling so bad here." Suddenly she grew scared. "What if that's what I've been transmitting instead of the signal? What will they think of me then."

She sat up and began to transmit the signal distinctly, clearly, repeating aloud to herself the code so as not to get muddled up. The roar of the planes' engines could be heard coming nearer and nearer.

Anti-aircraft guns opened fire.

"Aha, they don't like that!"

She stood up. She felt no pain, nothing. She pressed the key with all her strength as though it was not a signal she was transmitting but a command—"Wipe them out, wipe them out!"

Cleaving the inky darkness the first bomb came hurtling down with a crash. The air blast threw Mikhailova on her back. Golden splashes of flame were reflected in the puddles. The ground trembled from the dull thuds. The radio apparatus toppled down into the water. Mikhailova made an attempt to lift it up. Screaming bombs seemed to be making direct towards her, towards her pit.

She hunched up her shoulders and squatted down, closing her eyes tight. The glare from the flames penetrated through her eyelids. The blast of air following one explosion sent a pole with barbed wire around it flying into her pit. Between the bursting of the bombs she could hear the muffled sounds of things exploding and crashing at the aerodrome. The black mist reeked of gasoline.

And then came silence; the anti-aircraft guns ceased their fire.

"It's all over," she thought sadly to herself. "Now I'm alone again."

She tried to stand up, but her feet ... she could not feel them at all. What had happened? Then she grasped what was the matter. It happened sometimes that way. Temporary paralysis—the result of shellshock—that's all. She lay down with her face in the wet clay to rest a little. If only one bomb had come her way! How simple everything would have been. And then she would have been saved from the worst.

"No," she said suddenly to herself. "Others have been through worse and yet they've managed to come out of it. Nothing's going to happen to me. I don't want it to."

Somewhere not far off she could hear the chugging of a motorcar, and cold white beams of light flitted several times over the black shrubs; then came an explosion, something much weaker than that caused by a bomb, and then—quite near—several shots.

"They're looking for me. And how good it is just to lie like this. Won't I ever do this again?"

She made an attempt to turn over on her back but the pain in her foot was so intense that it seemed to lacerate her heart. She screamed, tried to scramble up and fell.

Cold, firm fingers unbuttoned her collar.

She opened her eyes.

"That you? You've come for me?"—Mikhailova said, and burst into tears.

The Captain brushed away her tears with his hand and she again closed her eyes. She could not walk. The Captain gripped her by the belt and pulled her out of the pit. His other hand hung limply at his side.

She could hear the runners of the sled scraping over the slush.

Then she saw the Captain. He was sitting on a tree stump holding one end of a strap between his teeth and binding his bare arm; blood trickled down from under the strap. Looking at Mikhailova the Captain asked:

"Well, how are you?"

"Pretty seedy," she whispered.

"Oh, well," the Captain said between his teeth, I'm

119

about done in. Try and make the distance yourself, it's not far from here."

"And how about you?"

"I'll stay here and have a bit of a rest."

The Captain tried to get up but with a queer sort of smile he slipped off the stump onto the ground. He was very heavy and it took Mikhailova a long time to drag his limp body onto the sled. He lay uncomfortably, face down, but to turn him onto his back was beyond her strength.

For a long time she tugged at the traces to make the sled move. Every step caused her unbearable pain. But she kept on tugging and walking backwards, dragging the sled over the slushy, soggy ground.

Everything seemed blurred. How long could she last. Why was she standing and not lying exhausted on the ground. Leaning against a tree she stood there, her eyes closed, afraid that her knees might give way because then, she knew, she would never have the strength to rise again.

She saw the Captain crawl off onto the ground; only his chest and head lay on the sled; he held on to the crossbar with his sound hand.

"It'll be much easier for you that way," he whispered.

He crawled along on his knees, half suspended over the sled. Sometimes he lost his grip and his face would strike the ground. When that happened she slid the sled under his chest, powerless to turn away so as not to look at his bruised and battered face.

Then she fell down and again she could hear the swish of the mud under the runners. Then she heard ice crackling. She felt as if she were suffocating, drowning; water closed over her. It seemed to her that all this was a dream.

She opened her eyes because she felt somebody's eyes fixed intently on her. The Captain was sitting on a bunk, emaciated, yellow, his beard unkempt, his hand in a sling between two dirty boards which served as splints. He was looking at her.

"You're awake," he said in a voice she didn't recognize.

"I wasn't sleeping."

"It makes no difference," he said. "It's just about the same."

She raised her arm and noticed that her arm was bare. "Did I undress myself?" she asked plaintively.

"I undressed you," the Captain said, and examining the fingers of his wounded arm he explained: "You and I had a bit of a dip in the river, and then I thought you were wounded."

"It makes no difference," she whispered and looked straight at him.

"That's true," he agreed.

She smiled and said:

"I knew you'd come back for me."

"How did you know?" the Captain asked with a smile.

"I simply knew."

"Nonsense," the Captain said, "You couldn't have known a thing. During the bombing you acted as an orientating point and, well, you might have been popped off, so I looked around and found a hayrick so as to be able to continue giving the signal by fire. And then again an armoured car fitted up with a radio apparatus detected your apparatus. It combed the whole place until I got it with a hand grenade. And thirdly...."

"What third?" Mikhailova asked merrily.

"And thirdly," the Captain went on in a serious tone of voice, "you're a good kid." And then he added sternly: "And generally speaking, have you ever heard of anybody acting otherwise in such circumstances?"

Mikhailova sat up and, holding a pile of clothes to her chest, she looked at the Captain with sparkling eyes and said loudly and distinctly:

"You know, I'm awfully fond of you."

The Captain turned away. His ears went red.

"Now, none of that."

"No, not that way.... I'm just simply fond of you," Mikhailova said proudly.

The Captain glanced at her, a frown on his face, and said thoughtfully:

"If that's what you mean, then, of course, it's different."

When the Captain returned to his unit from hospital his comrades did not recognize him. He was so jolly, so merry, so talkative. He laughed heartily, joked, and had a cheery word for everybody. But all the time his eyes kept searching for somebody. His comrades, noticing it, guessed whom and they told him offhand:

"By the way, you know Mikhailova is out again on a new job."

Bitter lines appeared on the Captain's face for an instant and disappeared. Without looking at anybody he said aloud so that everybody could hear:

"She's a good kid, there's no doubt about that," and adjusting his tunic he went off to report to his superior officer that he was back for duty.

Katya

KATYA NOVIKOVA is small and plump with a chubby face, rosy cheeks, fair hair cut in a boyish bob and black sparkling eyes. I can imagine that when she first showed up at the front her uniform must have been bulging in places and the girl must have looked pretty clumsy and comical. Now she is a smart, trim little soldier in top-boots which keep out the wet, and khaki tunic tucked in under a broad leather belt which she adjusts with the hand of a veteran. At her hip is a much worn holster from which protrudes the butt of a revolver that has seen good service. On the red tabs of her collar are four red triangles showing that she's a *Starshina*. This is equivalent to the rank of Sergeant-Major in foreign armies.

I heard about her exploits a long time before I made her acquaintance. I heard about them from people who could speak from first-hand knowledge. What interested me just now was how she would speak about herself. My assumption proved to be correct. Katya Novikova is a real heroine and has one thing in common with all real heroes whom I have chanced to meet, namely—extreme modesty. It is not sham modesty—the twin sister to hypocrisy. It is rather that restraint of an efficient person who is not fond of elaborating on his own affairs because he considers that what he does is just ordinary, everyday work, very hard work it is true, but nothing exceptional, and, consequently, something that can hardly be of interest to an outsider. To ram an enemy plane, direct one's blazing plane at a column of enemy gasoline oil tank cars, to slip through behind the enemy's lines and blow up a bridge—these are outstanding feats which are worth while telling about. And yet what Katya Novikova did at the front and what is being done by thousands of Russian boys and girls, is considered by them as being all in the day's work. It is this simple interpretation of their great mission that is real heroism.

On June 21, 1941, the graduating class of one of the Moscow shools gave a party. The boys and girls celebrated the fact that they had now become young men and young women.

"It was a splendid party," Katya said, "and I was having a really jolly time. We all of us conjured up visions of what we would be, discussed what university to study in. I had always wanted to be a flier and several times had handed in applications to one of the flying schools—but they would never accept me because I was so small. Yes, I'm a regular Tom Thumb and the boys and girls were cracking jokes at my expense that evening, and all of us were having a jolly time."

That night when the happy children who had suddenly become adults were sleeping their first adult sleep, thousands of bombs were sent hurtling on the country which had reared them, one hundred and eighty picked German divisions and thousands of tanks launched an attack on our peaceful cities, on our hearths and homes over which hovered the first hazy whisks of smoke, and parachute units, armed to the teeth, swooped down like gangsters from the skies. The war had begun.

The very next morning Katya Novikova, together with her bosom friend Lyolya, dashed to the nearest recruiting office to sign up as volunteers. They ran, clenching their small fists, and when they stood in front of the recruiting officer they could hardly say a word because they were out of breath and panting with emotion. They were not accepted in the army; they were advised to continue their studies. The girls joined a youth de-

124

tachment which was sent to dig anti-tank ditches and
build fortifications. When the detachment reached the
place where the field works had to be built the Germans
were already nearing Smolensk. Not far from where they
were a regiment took up its quarters en route to the
front. This regiment, apparently, was being held in reserve
by the High Command of the Western Front. It was the
end of July. Katya and Lyolya still cherished their dream
of enlisting. They bided their time, waiting for a suitable
opportunity. They were forever chatting with the Red Armymen, trying to pump them as to where regimental
headquarters were located. The girls harboured hopes that
once there they would be signed on in the regiment without any lengthy formalities. But not one of the men
would tell them where the staff headquarters were because
it was a military secret. The girls decided to resort to
cunning. They made straight for the place where the regiment was quartered. A sentry challenged them. They
paid no attention. He challenged them a second time.
Again they paid no attention but kept on their way, walking at a rapid pace. They were detained and sent under
escort to staff headquarters as suspicious characters. The
commander of the regiment laughed heartily at the in-
genuity of the girls who were bent on getting to the front
at all costs. He laughed, then he grew serious and, after
turning the matter over for a while, signed them on in
his regiment as Red Cross nurses. Uniforms and Red Cross
kit-bags were supplied to them. The next day the regiment left for the front and several hours later the girls
began to carry out their duties. The regiment on the
march was attacked by German dive bombers.

"I was simply terrified," Katya said, "and Lyolya and
I dashed into a field and lay flat on the ground because
that's what everybody did. Later on it turned out that it
wasn't so terrible after all because only a few men out
of the whole column were wounded. When we were at
school Lyolya and I learned to handle a machine-gun and

render first aid to the wounded. But the regimental commander told us to forget about a machine-gun.

"And when we began to render first aid to the wounded we realized that learning to do it is something entirely different from actually doing it at the front. Generally speaking, Lyolya and I are not of the sentimental kind. But here we saw real wounded people and we were so sorry for them, so sorry for them that we bandaged them and cried at the same time and could scarcely see a thing through our tears. Later on, too, we were always sorry for them but we didn't cry any more when we rendered them first aid. Only occasionally Lyolya and I cried to ourselves, at night, so that nobody should notice, because we saw so much suffering and at times, well, you can understand, we simply had to relieve our feelings by crying a little."

And so Katya Novikova began to see service at the front, the most terrible front the world has ever known. She was assigned to one of the battalions and always accompanied it when it went into action. She crawled on all fours with the infantry when it launched an attack and accompanied the men when they went out on patrol duty. Twice she was lightly wounded but refused to go to the rear. And so a month passed. She became accustomed to her work and, when all is said and done, was an excellent Red Cross nurse. The girls were very popular in the regiment.

"Everybody was forever asking us to join their particular unit," Katya said and burst out laughing. "The trench mortar crews would say to us: 'Join us, girls, and we'll teach you to handle a trench mortar.' The gunners, too, were always asking us to join them. The tankmen too. They were always saying: 'You'll ride with us in a tank; after all it'll be much nicer for you.' But Lyolya and I had one answer for them all: 'No, we're going to stick to the infantry.'"

The girls were simply dying to have revolvers. One day a wounded lieutenant whom Katya had carried to safety presented her with a revolver and three clips of cartridges.

"I got into hot water later on," Katya explained. "It was a slack day and Lyolya and I made for a certain crater to test the revolver. We had one in mind, a very big crater, made by a heavy explosive bomb. Well, we crawled down to the bottom of it so that nobody could see us, set up a bottle as a target and began to take potshots. We were so absorbed that we used up all three clips. And just then, you know, the alarm sounded because our men were under the impression that the Germans had penetrated our lines. We, of course, admitted our blunder. The regimental commander gave us such a dressing down, such a dressing down, something terrible! He took away my revolver and warned me that the next time he would have me demobilized."

During one attack the regimental commander was badly wounded in the right arm. He lost consciousness and Katya carried him off the battlefield. She was ordered to accompany him to Moscow, to the hospital. This she did and then decided to go for a walk. Proud as a peacock she strolled about her own dear Moscow, dressed in full military kit, thinking all the time how nice it would be to meet some of her old friends, and just then whom should she meet but Lusya.

"And Lusya, you know, was racking her brains all the time how to get to the front and when she caught sight of me she became terribly excited. 'How did you manage to get to the front?' she asked. I told her how I wangled it, what I was doing there, how I had just brought back the regimental commander, that I had a car and a chauffeur at my disposal and that I was returning to my unit the next day. Lusya says to me: 'Katya, you've got to take me with you.' She was so excited that she simply could not stand still. She's not a bit like me. Tall, slim, a real peach. And graceful! She's much older than me. She had already turned twenty and had graduated from the university. I said to her: 'Don't be silly, Lusya. How can I take you with me? What do you think, it's so easy to get to the front? Our documents will be examined about a hundred times on the way.' Well, we thought and thought and this is what we decided to do. We went to the hospital to our regimental commander and tried our best to pursuade him. Well, he, of course, knew that we girls weren't doing such bad work in his regiment. And with his left hand— his right hand, you know, was wounded—wrote an order that Lusya was to be signed on in the regiment as a nurse. The next morning we left together and we were so happy that we sang all the way."

There were now three Red Cross nurses in the regiment and they were each assigned to a separate battalion. They went through thick and thin, their hands grew rough and coarse. They fulfilled the work assigned to them— crawling from one man to another, rendering first aid to the wounded. When they heard somebody call out: "Ambulance," they would look for the man and make their way to him. The regiment was advancing and every day cut several hundred metres deeper into the German lines of defence. The girls were so busy that they hardly ever met.

"One day," Katya said, "some presents were brought to the regiment and we met near the regimental headquarters. For the three of us there was one apple, true, an enormous apple—like this—and a pair of thin stockings, a gorgeous pair. You know—the real expensive sort. We, of course, didn't so much as hint to each other but we were all of us simply dying to try them on because, after all, we're girls. And we held those gorgeous stockings in our hands, so soft and silky and it seemed so funny to look at them. I said: 'You take them, Lusya, because, after all, you're the eldest and the best looker.' And Lusya says: 'You're crazy, Katya. We've got to share them somehow.' We laughed and laughed and cut them up into three parts and each of us made a pair of socks out of them and wore them on the top of our puttees. And the apple we also cut into three parts and ate it. Well, after that we spent the evening together and talked of old times. And Lusya said at the time: 'Look here, girls, let's make a pledge that each of us kills five Germans because I'm certain that, in the long run, we'll get into the fighting ranks.' We made a solemn pledge and kissed each other on parting. It's a good thing we did because I never saw Lusya again. The regiment launched an attack the next day and Lusya was killed. She was very badly wounded by a bomb. She was carried off behind the lines for about a half a mile. Just then she came to and saw several ambulance men standing around her, everybody was so sorry for her, you know. She looked at them and called out: 'What are you standing here for? There's fighting going on over there—go on, get busy.' She died with those words on her lips. I got to know about it later on. It was a day which changed my whole destiny because that morning I was finally taken on as a regular."

This is what happened to Katya that day. The regiment was advancing. One of our machine-guns took up a position on the right flank and combed the woods where German automatic-riflemen were concentrating. Suddenly the machine-gun ceased firing.

"Well, I crawled, of course, towards the machine-gunner thinking that he was wounded. I crawled up to him and saw that he had been killed; he was sprawling over the machine-gun, his hands gripping the trigger. I unclasped his fingers from the machine-gun and at once made ready to open fire. Just then the battalion commander crawled up: 'What are you up to, Katya?' he asked. I was scared stiff because I thought he wouldn't let me open fire. I said to him: 'Comrade Captain! I learned how to handle a machine-gun in school.' He says to me: 'All right, give it to them for all you're worth, Katya. Fire away, comb those woods.' I said—'That's just what I was about to do.' 'Right you are,' he says, 'go ahead, give it to them hot.' We got those Germans out of the woods and did our regiment attack! We occupied the village. When we got to the village graveyard the Germans opened a raking fire with their heavy guns. The shells came thick and fast. I don't remember another such bombardment. The shells simply ploughed up the ground. The bodies of the buried went flying out of the graves and it was impossible to tell which had been killed and when. I hid my head under my machine-gun. We stuck it though. And after that we launched forward again. Lugging that machine-gun along was rather difficult. I wasn't used to it then. But later on I got used to it."

For over a month Katya was a machine-gunner and considerably exceeded the plan that Lusya had proposed. She was an excellent machine-gunner, with a good eye and splendid judgment.

In September Katya was badly shellshocked and sent to hospital in Moscow. They kept her there until November. When she was signed out she received a certificate stating that she was unfit for military service and was directed to the civil authorities to continue her education.

"But how can one think of education when we've got to smash the Germans?" Katya said with a grim smile. "I was terribly down in the mouth. I didn't even know where my regiment was quartered. What was I to do? I looked around and finally signed up in a parachute squad as an automatic-rifleman."

"How did you manage to do it, Katya?" I asked, "what with that certificate of yours from the hospital."

"I didn't show them that one. I showed them something else—a document I received from the regiment."

It was an excellent document. It stated that Katya had served first as a Red Cross nurse and subsequently as a machine-gunner and that for her bravery she had been recommended for a decoration.

It's pleasant to possess a document like that. When I read it Katya blushed and felt somewhat embarrassed.

"To make a long story short I was accepted," she said. "Now we're undergoing a special course of training. There's a rumour that we'll be off to the front soon."

Stout Heart

H^E stood there in front of the Captain—snub-nosed, high cheekboned, in an overcoat sizes too small for him with a collar of imitation beaver. His nose was red from the dry, piercing wind that swept the steppes. His blue, chapped lips trembled, but his dark eyes looked searchingly and almost sternly at the Captain.

His footgear was far from suitable to the weather— grey canvas shoes, frayed at the toes.

The Captain read the note which the staff headquarters had sent with an orderly: "... detained this morning at the forward positions... claims that for two weeks he reconnoitred the German forces in the vicinity of sovkhoz... sending him on to you since his information might be of use to the battery...."

The Captain folded the note and put it into the breast pocket of his fur-lined tunic.

"What's your name?"

The youngster pulled himself together, threw back his head and attempted to click his heels before replying, but his lips twisted with pain and he said hurriedly:

"Nikolai Vikhrov, Comrade Captain."

The Captain glanced at the youngster's shoes and shook his head.

"Those pumps of yours are a bit out of season, Comrade Vikhrov. Your feet must be frozen."

The youngster stood there with downcast eyes. With an effort he kept back the tears that welled up in them. The

9*

Captain wondered how he had managed to make his way across the steppes at night in such shoes and in such a bitter frost. The very thought sent a cold shiver down his spine. He patted the boy's shoulders.

"Come on. Come along to my den. It's warmer there and we'll have a chat."

A fire was burning merrily in the stove inside the commander's casemate. The youngster stood on the threshold looking around the room.

"Take your things off," the Captain said. "It's hot in here, just like the beach at Artek. Warm yourself up."

The youngster took off his threadbare coat and folding it neatly with the lining outside stood on his tiptoes and hung it up on top of the Captain's tunic. Without his coat the youngster was terribly thin. "He must have had a hard time of it," the Captain thought.

"Sit down. First we'll have a snack and then we'll settle down to business. Do you like strong tea?"

The Captain poured the tea out for him in his own mug. "Here, put some sugar into it."

He motioned to a segment of a six-inch shell case filled to the brim with sparkling snow-white lumps of sugar.

The youngster glanced at him somewhat queerly. His thin face began to twitch and big childish tears which he could not restrain rolled down his cheeks onto the table. The Captain sighed, moved nearer to the lad and put his arm around his thin shoulders.

"Now, now," he said caressingly. "Now, that's all right. Forget about what happened. Here nobody will hurt you."

The youngster dashed aside his tears with a quick and embarrassed movement.

"It ... it's nothing ... Comrade Captain," he said sheepishly. "It wasn't of myself but of my Mama I was thinking."

"Oh, I see," the Captain drawled, "your Ma. Well, cheer up, my lad, we'll get your Ma out too. She's alive is she?"

132

"Uh-huh," the boy's eyes lighted up with a tender look, "only it's pretty hungry in our district. Mama used to collect the potato peelings in the German kitchen at night. The sentry caught her once. He hit her over the arm with his rifle butt. She can't bend it to this day."

He clenched his teeth. The tender look vanished from his eyes. Now they gleamed hard and dry. The Captain stroked his hair.

"Lie down and have a rest."

The youngster looked at him appealingly.

"Later on ... I don't want to sleep just yet. I want to tell you about them first."

A stubborn, passionate note rang in his voice and the Captain did not insist. He sat down at the other end of the table and took out a notebook.

"Very well. Fire away. How many Germans do you think there are in the sovkhoz?"

The youngster answered rapidly, without hesitation:

"A battalion of infantry. The 175th Regiment. Bavarians."

The Captain was surprised at the explicity of the reply and looked searchingly at his young guest.

"How do you know?"

"They have the figures on their shoulder straps. And I remembered it. Then there's the motorcyclists. A company of them. A squad of medium tanks. In the bunkers there are field guns and anti-tank guns. They've strongly fortified the place, Comrade Captain. Trucks have been bringing up cement all the time. I watched them through the window."

"Can you tell me where those bunkers are?" the Captain asked leaning forward. He suddenly sensed that confronting him was not an ordinary, naive child but a sharp-eyed, intelligent and efficient scout.

"Their largest bunker is near the melon plot, just beyond the old threshing barn.... And the other...."

"Here, wait a minute," the Captain interrupted him.

133

"It's fine that you remember it all so well. But understand that we don't come from your sovkhoz. Where the melon plot is or the threshing barn we don't know. And a ten-inch naval gun, my boy, is a powerful toy. If we start letting fly just on chance then we may do an enormous amount of damage before we hit the target. And there are our people there.... And your mother too...."

The youngster looked at the Captain and asked in surprise:

"But haven't you got any maps, Comrade Captain?"

"I have maps, all right.... Do you know anything about maps?"

The youngster smiled with a sort of condescending superiority.

"Why, of course.... My Dad's a geodesist. I can draw maps too. My Dad's also a commander now," he added with pride.

"Upon my soul, you're worth your weight in gold, my boy," the Captain said laughingly, unfolding a large-scale map on the table.

The youngster, kneeling on a chair, bent over the map. There was an animated look on his face as his finger moved over the map to a point under which was marked: *"Sovkhoz Novy Put."*

"Here it is," he said smiling happily, "as clear as can be. What a splendid map you've got. And so many details—just like a chart.... Here to the East—this is where the old threshing barn is."

He found his orientation on the map unerringly, like an experienced topographer, and very soon a whole palisade of red crosses made by the Captain's pencil appeared in all directions, indicating various targets. The Captain was satisfied.

"Excellent, Kolya." And the Captain approvingly patted the youngster's skinny shoulders. The boy for a moment ceased to be a scout and in a childish way pressed his cheek against the palm of the Captain's hand. The caress turned him into a child again. The Captain folded up the map.

"And now, Comrade Vikhrov, discipline demands that you immediately go to sleep."

The boy did not protest. The food and the warmth had made him sleepy, he could hardly keep his eyes open or stop yawning. The Captain put him to bed, covered him with his own blanket, tucked him in and sat down again at the table to calculate the range. He was so absorbed in his work that he did not notice how the time flew by. A voice called him softly, interrupting him at his work.

"Comrade Captain—what time is it, please?"

The boy was sitting up in bed with a worried look on his face.

"Now you go to sleep," the Captain said kindly. "What do you want to know the time for?" I'll wake you up right enough when we get going."

The boy's face clouded. Again that stubborn note sounded in his voice:

"No, no. I have to get back. I promised Mama I would. She'll be worrying, thinking I'm killed. I'll be off as soon as it gets dark."

The Captain was nonplussed. The thought never entered his head that the youngster was really bent on repeating a second time the terrible journey he had made over the steppes at night—a road he had managed to make once by luck.

"Nonsense," the Captain said angrily. "Who'll let you go? Even if you do manage to slip through the German lines you'll come under the fire of our guns there, in the sovkhoz."

The youngster knit his brows and went red to the roots of his hair:

"I'll get by the Germans, all right. It's so cold at night that they sit indoors. And I know all the ways and byways by heart.... Please, do let me go."

He begged so earnestly and persistently that for a moment the thought flashed through the Captain's mind: "And what if everything the youngster has been telling me is only just claptrap?" But looking at those clear, childish eyes he immediately discarded the thought.

"You know, Comrade Captain, the Germans don't allow anybody to leave the sovkhoz. If they find out I'm gone Mama'll be made to suffer...."

"Very well." The Captain took out his watch. "It's now 4.30. Let's go along to the observation post first and check up everything again. As soon as it gets dark we'll let you through the lines. Only be careful. Take care of yourself."

At the forward observation post the Captain sat down at one of the range finders. In the evening mist covering the snow-swept steppes it was just possible to make out in the distance several dark specks—the sovkhoz buildings. The Captain turned to the youngster and beckoned to him.

"Here, take a look, maybe you can see your Ma...."

Kolya smiled appreciatingly and put his eye to the glass. The Captain slowly turned the small wheel regulating the horizontal sight, giving the youngster a panorama of the place he had come from. Suddenly, Kolya jumped up and all excited tugged the Captain by the sleeve.

"Look! You can see the dove-cot. That's mine, Comrade Captain. Really and truly."

The Captain bent down over the range finder. In his field of vision, towering above the leafless poplars, above the green roofs with patches of rust on them, he could see a tiny box on top of a mast. The Captain could make it out quite clearly. The sight of it suddenly gave him an idea. Taking Kolya by the arm he led him away to one side and, much to the surprise of the naval gunners, carried on an animated conversation with him in a whisper.

"D'you understand?" the Captain asked and Kolya, his eyes sparkling roguishly, nodded his head. It grew dark.

The Captain saw Kolya as far as the outpost. And when the youngster, accompanied by two seamen, disappeared in the dusk the Captain stood there for a long time listening anxiously to hear whether there were any shots.

Before dawn he was back again at the observation post, and as soon as he could distinguish the small square black patch of the dove-cot against the grey sky—he gave the order. The first salvo—to straddle the range—pierced the silence of the early morn.

The rumbling of the guns echoed through the hills. The Captain saw the dark square patch on top of the mast rock twice and after a pause, once more.

"Wide of the mark . . . to the right," he interpreted the signal to himself and the Captain gave the order for the second salvo. This time the dove-cot did not move and the Captain gave three volleys from both batteries. With the animation of a veteran gunner he saw logs and slabs of cement flying skywards through the clouds of smoke. The Captain laughed to himself and set a new range. And again the dove-cot conducted a tête-à-tête with him. This time the fire was directed where the map indicated the location of the ammunition dump and oil tanks. The first salvo hit the target fair and square. A wide strip of pale, devouring flames flared up on the horizon. Everything disappeared in a cloud of smoke—trees, roofs, the mast with the dove-cot on top of it. The explosion was so powerful that the Captain with alarm thought of the youngster.

The telephone rang. The outpost requested the guns to cease fire. The infantry was launching an attack. The Captain jumped into the side car of a motorcycle and dashed across country towards the outpost. The rattling of the machine-guns and the bursting of hand grenades could be heard from the sovkhoz. The Germans, taken by surprise and having lost their main defences, put up a weak resistance. From the outskirts of the village brightly coloured flags signalled that the enemy was retreating. The Captain dashed across the steppes in a direct line. A greyish-white cloud of smoke given out by the burning gasoline flitted over the sovkhoz orchards; bursting shells thudded dully. The Captain hastened towards a green roof hemmed in between some shattered poplars. From a distance he saw the figure of a woman wrapped up in a shawl standing at the gate. A small boy was standing at her side holding her hand. She ran out to meet the Captain and the latter, catching hold of Kolya, lifted him up and hugged him. But the youngster just then did not wish to be considered a small boy. He tore himself loose from the Captain's embrace and bringing up his hand smartly to his tattered cap in a salute, he reported:

"Comrade Captain, scout Nikolai Vikhrov has carried out your orders!"

The woman who came up had a harassed look in her eyes and with a tired smile on her lips she stretched out her hand to the Captain.

"How do you do.... He's been waiting for you so.... We have all been waiting for you. You cannot imagine how thankful we are."

She curtsied to the Captain in the dear old Russian style. Kolya stood alongside the Captain.

"Excellent. You did a splendid job, my boy.... Weren't you terrified up on that attic when we began firing?" the Captain asked.

Kolya looked at him simply, trustingly.

"I was. I was terribly afraid, Comrade Captain. When the first shells burst the house began to rock and I was certain that it was going to cave in. I nearly did a bunk from the attic. And then I grew ashamed of myself. I kept on saying to myself: 'Sit tight, sit tight, sit tight.' And I stayed there until the ammunition dump exploded. And after that I don't seem to remember how I managed to get down."

He hid his face sheepishly against the Captain's tunic—this thirteen-year-old hero, a small Russian boy with a stout heart, the heart of his people.

The Surgeon

THE WOUNDED were brought in at night and after
the darkness, the drizzling rain, the short run in the
Red Cross car from the station and the feeling of depression to which people who have lost their usual equanimity fall prey, they were confronted by the efficient
and ordered life of the hospital.

It was three o'clock in the morning when the doctor
approached the second lieutenant's bed. He had been badly wounded in the thigh and in the elbow. The wound
had only just been dressed. The dressing had been very
painful. He lay awake on his back with his eyes wide open
and looked at the dark corner of the ward with an intent
and strained look as though there, as on a screen, he
could retrace the twenty-two years of his life. Beads of
perspiration stood out on his forehead and the skin on his
face and hands grew dry and tawny as it usually does
when people have suffered from loss of blood and vitality.

The doctor, a stocky little man in pince-nez with
thick lenses, in a well laundered white surgeon's coat
which, nevertheless, showed traces of his work, felt the
white finger tips of the wounded man with an experienced
touch. Carefully pressing each finger he found the frail
line of life which still flickered in the mutilated, powerless hand. The second lieutenant turned his tired eyes
which had so suddenly become old and looked at the haggard, almost bloodless face of the doctor which showed
the strain under which he had been these last sleepless

nights and days, at the thin stubble on his chin, at the thick lenses of his pince-nez which hid the real expression in his eyes.

"Tell me, please, doctor," he said, "I suppose my arm's gone? The way that blasted bomb crippled me!"

He wanted to say something more but he turned his face away to hide the tears so entirely out of place in a man who had been through the thick of it.

"First we'll get that wound of yours healed and then we'll see," the doctor replied in a business-like, professional manner, which masked all signs of compassion. "We'll discuss that subject another time."

He moved on to the next wounded man who met him with sad and penetrating eyes. It was three o'clock in the morning and the operation room, flooded with light, was ready for the morning round of operations. The second lieutenant, his heavy arm across his chest, was alone again. His face with the resolute lines of a man whom stern trials had prematurely brought to manhood, took on a boyish look, the same, perhaps, as it had borne when the war broke out. His arm, of course, was crippled for good. Here it was lying on his chest, numb, somebody else's; never again would it bend at the elbow. Again he looked at the dark corner of the ward as though critically analysing his short life. Of course, in comparison with the misfortunes that had befallen thousands of other human lives what, in fact, could his own, small misfortune mean? But it was here, part and parcel of him, in that inanimate lump swathed in bandages which had once been his right arm with its numb, dead fingers. And then, as always happens during sickness, various odd things began to flit through his mind. What a tired look there was on the doctor's pallid face. Apparently, he had not slept for days on end. It would be interesting to know whether he took off those pince-nez of his with the thick lenses when he was operating. Yes, it was the kind of glass that aquariums are usually made of. Probably all the telescopes he had bought for his younger brothers at that store the Zoological Gardens had on Kuznetsky Street in Moscow were smashed. He fell asleep.

Morning came, and with it the measured tread of life in the hospital with its hopes and chagrins of hundreds of people who had just been brought in or who had already been returned to life—life which flowed on beyond the windows in the rustling of the leaves, glowed in the flowers on the table and triumphed, in spite of everything . . . . Man, brought back from oblivion after an operation, desired to live. The ward was suddenly flooded with the white glare of a summer's day; a sparrow alighted on a lilac bush outside the window and swayed to and fro trimming its feathers, and everyone looked at it so tenderly and recalled their childhood, springtime in their own home-towns when the sparrows began to chirrup, and with it came the urge to live which no suffering could smother.

During the day the second lieutenant was again taken to the dressing room and at night, when the clock struck three, the small stocky doctor of yesterday again approached his bed.

"Here we are again," he said and with cautious movements began to feel the tips of the second lieutenant's fingers. "The night, my friend, is for sleep." He sat down on the bed, ignoring in his professional way the tears of weakness in the lieutenant's eyes. "What did you do before the war?" he asked.

"I was an engraver," the lieutenant replied, "I engrave on wood."

He saw now, close at hand, the tired, anæmic face of the doctor and the pale, weak, near-sighted eyes behind the thick lenses, blue—almost like a baby's.

"Yes, for such a profession one needs one's fingers," the doctor said stroking and bending the upper joints of the dead hand. "Well, I think we'll be able to give you back your fingers. Your arm will not bend at the elbow

141

—nothing can be done. . . . An elbow joint cannot be replaced. But as far as your fingers are concerned they'll function all right."

"Is that really possible, doctor?" the lieutenant asked. His forehead grew damp but this time from an overwhelming joy that left him weak. "And here was I thinking that they would never be of any more use."

"We'll train them little by little, accustom them to move," the doctor said, still carefully working on the wounded arm. "Yes, your fingers will come to life."

A solitary night lamp burned in the ward and the sufferings of the inmates, their hopes and chagrins and joys—all was locked in slumber, the heavy slumber of pain which makes itself felt even in sleep, or the light, refreshing sleep of those on the road to convalescence. And the lieutenant, too, suddenly felt as if he was being wafted away, the bed under him seemed to hover in space and he fell into a forgetfulness, attributing all this to weakness and dizziness. Then he again came back. The doctor was still sitting near him, on his bed. With trained, jerky movements he stroked and bent the paralysed, as it were, fingers. He took off his pince-nez and his eyes, like the eyes of all near-sighted people, were gentle; and the lieutenant suddenly saw that he was dozing and he understood how tired the doctor must be before his day was over.

"Better have a rest, doctor," he said to him, "never mind my fingers. . . . How many operations you must have made today!"

The doctor bent and unbent the fingers several times more.

"It's true," he replied, a smile suddenly lighting up his face, "I've done more than enough operations for one day. As for taking a rest, I'll do that when the war's over. Now try and sleep. . . . Sleep, you know, is the best of all medicine and can do more for you than we doctors."

He covered him up with the sheet, right up to his

chin, in the way his mother used to tuck him in when he was a youngster, took his pince-nez with the thick lenses from the table and moved on. For the first time after two weeks of pain the lieutenant fell into a sound, invigorating sleep. The breeze coming in through the open window lightly touched his brow, the trees rustled in the garden and the air was fragrant with the freshness of a summer's night and with life which triumphs over the sufferings of all people.

The next night the doctor came to see him again; the lieutenant was not sleeping—he was waiting for him.

"So you see how things are, lieutenant," the doctor said as though continuing the conversation which had been interrupted the night before. He again sat down next to him on the bed, took his arm into his own hands, the hands, of a surgeon, stained with iodine and with the nails cut very short, almost to the quick. "We'll hope for the best and only for the very best. What were you doing by the way, book illustrations or what?"

"Yes, I've only done several children's books so far.... Hans Anderson's Fairy Tales. You remember '*The Ugly Duckling*'?"

"Of course, I do. I have good cause to remember it," he said with a smile. "When I was at school they used to tease me, they nicknamed me ugly duckling.... You see, I'm not what you'd call handsome...."

"You ... doctor," the lieutenant began, but what he wanted to say might have sounded so femininely exultant that he felt ashamed and said nothing.

Again with measured movements, almost falling asleep from fatigue, he massaged the wounded hand and it seemed to the lieutenant that his fingers were beginning to live. They were not alive yet but now he believed they would be soon. Again that blessed forgetfulness wafted him away, away to his forgotten youth, to the box-wood board which he would engrave, to the smell of wood which had become a part of his life, to his set of chisels

143

and knives.... There, it stood, on the shore of the lake, an ugly duckling, a pathetically tender being with a human heart, a fairy tale which had been a part of his childhood, and the swans bowed their subtle necks before it and stroked its feathers with their beaks....

"That'll do for today," the doctor said putting on his pince-nez and the lieutenant realized that it was only during these minutes that he had an opportunity of resting his tired eyes. "And now it's time for you to sleep."

And again he moved away down the ward, and further on down the corridor at the end of which the operating room, flooded with light, was being prepared for the morning round of operations.

During the third week the lieutenant, for the first time, began to move his fingers. They still did not seem his own but they were already alive. He looked at them and they answered him by moving. This was a long-lost feeling, something similar, perhaps, to that first word one pronounces in childhood. The doctor came at night again and the lieutenant's fingers for the first time replied to the doctor's fingers. The doctor squeezed them and again they answered him.

"So you see, Lieutenant," the doctor said with animation, "your fingers are alive. You will be able to draw and engrave your boards.... Of course, you'll have to get accustomed to it."

The lieutenant lay still and silent, his eyes on the corner of the ward as then, on that first day.

"Why are you silent? You should be happy," the doctor said looking searchingly at his averted face. "You see, the massage has helped you after all."

"You have given me all your spare time, doctor... and you have so little of it," he said after a pause. "And how, and in what way can I ever thank you?" And he recalled the long night hours and the gloom of the sleeping ward and those childlike, short-sighted eyes without the pince-nez, and the laundered white surgeon's coat with a spot

144

or two of blood on it and that brisk way he fought off weariness and sleep.

"A doctor has no spare time," he said, still carefully but vigorously massaging the fingers of the lieutenant's hand that had been brought back to life. "And particularly a surgeon, and with a war on. A human life saved—that's the best thanks for our labours. But if you want to thank me you can, by the way," he added suddenly. "Send me the first drawing you make with this hand of yours.... You know, even though it may be an 'ugly duckling.' "

And he squeezed the lieutenant's fingers and they responded to his clasp and, satisfied, he moved on down the half-darkened ward. The lieutenant was again alone. He lay on his back and his arm, come to life, lay warm across his chest. It seemed to him that only now had the inspiration of the artist come to him and that his mutilated, wounded arm was now, perhaps, destined to achieve what actually was his goal in life.

Life

SHE was crossing the street with her four-year-old boy. Two street-cars which had stopped at both ends of the crossroads barred the way. She waited for them to pass.

Suddenly the youngster, whooping with joy, tore away from his mother and dashed across the street right in front of the street-cars which had already begun to move.

The mother shrieked. Her cry was so terrifying that both street-car drivers simultaneously applied their brakes. The people in the cars looked out of the windows to see what was the matter while those hanging onto the steps began to peer under the wheels.

"There's a mother for you!" women exclaimed from every side. "She ought to be ashamed of herself."

She rushed horror-stricken towards the narrow space between the two street-cars, calling: "Kolya! Kolya!" and almost instantaneously her whole appearance became miserable and woebegone.

"What's your boy like? In a blue blouse? A fair-haired youngster?"

Unable to speak, wiping the sweat away that streamed down her face, one hand clasped to her throat, she nodded her head, looking at the people around her with eyes wide open with horror.

"Is that your boy? Look! A military man snatched him up. He's most likely hurt...."

"Where? Where?" and she hastened in the direction they indicated.

A tall airman, covered with dust from head to foot, so much so that he seemed to be dressed in some grey uniform, was walking down the street with Kolya in his arms, hugging him and kissing him. The boy was laughing happily, pulling the airman's ear. He did not seem to be hurt in any way. And he seemed to enjoy being in the airman's arms.

"Comrade airman, comrade airman, are you crazy, or what?" the mother shouted running after him.

But he walked on, apparently not having heard a word.

"Kolya, my own little Kolya," he kept on muttering as though in a trance. "How did you come to be here, you little imp?"

The boy was telling him something.

"How dare you?" The mother clutched the airman by the arm and stopped him. She was almost on the verge of hysterics.

"Where are you taking my boy?" she almost shouted. "This is outrageous! Let him go at once! I'll call a militiaman!"

The airman glanced at her in bewilderment.

"What do you want?" he asked the woman.

A crowd began to collect.

"Where are you taking my boy? This is outrageous!"

"Your boy? He's my son," and as though to convince himself the airman looked in surprise at the youngster. "Who's boy are you, Kolya?"

"Your's, Daddy," the youngster replied and, stretching out his hand towards the woman, he said: "and she's Mama."

"Whose Mama? Where's your Mama?"

"My real Mama is in the grave," Kolya explained "The Germans, when they came, they shot her and Aunty Lipa put her hand over my eyes, but later on I had a look...."

"That'll do, Kolya, that'll do," and the father convulsively drew a deep breath. "So you took him. Was it long ago?" he asked, turning to the woman.

She stood there her eyes half-closed, biting her lip as though trying to overcome some acute pain. Her hand which she still held clasped to her throat was trembling.

"Look here," the airman said, "you had better pull yourself together. What's to be done?... You and I had better talk things over.... Where were you going?"

"Home."

"To your flat?"

"Why, of course, to our home." And she nodded timidly in the direction of the boy.

"Well, come on. True, I look like the devil knows what.... And here I land into such a complicated affair.... But never mind."

The crowd slowly made room for them.

"That's nothing.... This way.... Kolya, where is your handkerchief? Wipe your nose.... To the right.... But you cannot, you must not, you dare not do anything that would be against the law."

He did not say anything. She walked after him with such a guilty look on her face as if she had been caught red-handed in some crime for which the most severe punishment awaited her.

They did not remember how they reached the place.

It was a tiny little room, poorly furnished, with a sofa, a small table and an oil stove in one of the corners fixed up on a suitcase.

Several old toys were lying about on the windowsill.

The airman put his son down on the floor.

"Well, permit me to introduce myself. I'm Major Brazhnev."

"My name is Rogalchuk. I'm very pleased to meet you. I do hope there'll be no misunderstanding between us."

"What kind of misunderstanding can there be?" he asked in surprise, looking sternly at this woman who made a slightly unpleasant impression on him.

148

She was below average height, rather thin, with a pleasant enough face, spoiled by the heavy lines round her mouth and an expression of extreme bewilderment, sadness, unhappiness, stamped all over her face.

Her long hair was plaited around her head in a golden braid. Her arms were thin, of a bluish tinge. Anæmic.

"Sit down, please," he said. "We'd better talk things over. I haven't much time."

"Don't you think you'd better have a wash and brush up first, Comrade Brazhnev? And perhaps a cup of tea?..."

In the woman's voice the Major thought he sensed a desire to detain him, to make a request, beg something of him.

"No, let's talk things over first."

Before beginning her narrative, however, she slipped out of the room to one of the neighbours and from sounds in the corridor Brazhnev guessed that a kettle had been put on.

"I used to live in Leningrad," Rogalchuk said. "My husband was killed in January, almost in front of my eyes. I was left alone. It was such a blow to me that I did not know whether I would be able to go on living. I had to have some live being near me whose life, whose well-being ... whose happiness depended on me. I decided to adopt an orphan. There are so many of them. But I did not find one at once. I looked for somebody who would resemble my husband. True, children change in time, but I felt in need, at least for a month or so, of seeing the dear features in the face of the little one. And then I also wanted the boy's name to be the same as his. When I first saw Kolya I immediately realized that he was what I was looking for, my boy, mine forever."

"But he's no orphan," the Major said. "It's a mistake."

"Yes, Daddy, I am an orphan," Kolya butted in. "Aunty Lipa was also killed by the Germans."

He sat there, such a tiny tot, pale, his face streaked with the thin blue veins which stood out clearly under the skin, attentively following the unraveling of his own life.

"In the orphanage I was told that Kolya's mother had been killed, that his father had been killed at the front, that his nearest relatives had also either been killed or were lying wounded in hospital. I immediately settled all formalities and took him."

"It wasn't I who was killed at the time, but someone of the same name," the Major said.

Rogalchuk glanced around the room with a worried look as though she was searching for something.

"What are you looking for, Mama?" the boy asked.

"Where is my handbag, dear?"

"Again you can't see anything, Mama. There it is on the chair."

The Major glanced furtively at his son, drumming on the table with his fingers.

It stung him to the quick to hear his boy call this strange woman Mama, but he felt unable to rebuke him for it.

Rogalchuk took her passport out of her handbag and placed it in front of the Major.

"I was firmly convinced that I had every right to adopt the son of a Red Army commander who had been killed in action. I assure you that my education, training and the means I have are quite sufficient to bring up the boy.... I too, am the widow of a Red Army commander."

She had a low but pleasant voice and listening to it Brazhnev thought of that other woman—who had sparkled with wit, who, too, had been somewhat frail but, still, much stronger than this woman—the woman he would never see again, who had been his wife and in whom his happiness, his hopes, his very life had been bound up.

It seemed to him that with her death he had lost a part of his own self, that he had become some vulnerable mortal, without any prospects, as though with her he had lost a part of his own, vast, seemingly unbounded future.

A neighbour brought in a tray on which there were two cups of tea and a small saucer of syrup. Brazhnev absent-mindedly took one of the cups and only after he had put two teaspoonfuls of syrup in it did he realize that he was doing the wrong thing.

Silence reigned in the room. Rogalchuk, apparently, had told him all there was to be told.

"Papa, papa, what have you done? And you so big"—and Kolya, overjoyed that he had caught his father doing something he should not have done, clapped his hands. "And won't Mama give it to you! Don't you know that you must always smear your syrup on the bread?"

His father smiled sheepishly.

"Have I put my foot in it? I seem to have got out of the way of things.... Sorry, I won't do it again. Put some into your tea, Kolya."

"That's not the right thing to do," the youngster said in the tone of a mentor. "I have to eat my porridge first and after that I'll have my tea."

"You, apparently, were not listening to me," Rogalchuk said, her voice trembling with emotion. "Well, listen: Kolya is as much my son as he is yours. He is my son before the law. I adopted him."

"What do you mean you adopted him? I must say ..."

"Of course, he is Nikolai Brazhnev. But he has been registered on my passport."

The Major got up and began to pace the room.

"Here's the devil of a situation," he said. "Whatever shall we do? And we have to decide at once. And we have to decide sensibly. First of all I want to give you my heartfelt thanks for having looked after my boy, for the tender care and love you have given him. You cannot imagine how thankful I am, and for the fight you are putting up for him. Had I found him a homeless waif I'm sure I don't know what I should have done. Really, it would have been a calamity.... Well, what shall we do when I get back after the war?"

"Why think about it just now," Rogalchuk replied firmly. "I think when the time comes we shall decide matters so that the boy stands to gain and not to lose.'"

Never was the boy so dear to him as now. In his patched shirt, made over from an old blouse, he looked so terribly worried. He understood that his fate was being decided and, perhaps, he was afraid that the adults would not decide it in the proper way.

The Major heaved a sigh.

"How about your income—is it enough for two?"

"I can't complain."

Rogalchuk calmed down somewhat, her face lit up.

"And how about clothes—it must be rather difficult nowadays."

"He has what is most essential. This is not the time for luxuries. And, then again, he's not a spoiled child, he's very serious minded."

"Of course, I'll make you an allowance from my pay. And what's more you'll have to get attached to the Army and Navy Store. Yes, we'll do that. You haven't a pencil, have you? Write down my field post office number."

Rogalchuk wrote down the address.

"Well, perhaps, now, you'll have a wash and brush up?" she asked. "Here's a basin and some water."

"Thank you very much. I'm not taking up your time, am I?"

"No, it's my day off today."

"Mama promised to take me to the movies today," Kolya said. "You come, too, Papa."

"I can't, my boy. I'll see you as far as the movies,

152

but I'm afraid I have no time for that just now. I have to be off."

Rogalchuk left the room so as not to embarrass the Major in any way. The Major stripped to the waist and washed. After that he took Rogalchuk's passport which was lying on the table and began to examine it carefully. He was reading it when she entered the room.

"So you're Zinaida Antonovna," he said somewhat embarrassed. "Well, well. . . . I'm Vasili Vasilyevich. I'm thirty-six. I suppose we'd better be acquainted. What do you think?"

"I think so too," she said with a smile.

The Major brushed his tunic and with a handkerchief he cleaned the dust from the decorations pinned to it.

"Well, it's time for me to be going," he said.

They went out together, holding the boy by the hand.

Tall, tanned, the Major with two decorations pinned on his chest, attracted the attention of all the youngsters in the neighbourhood. They stopped and looked at him, their mouths gaping. Kolya walked between them, proud and happy.

At the street-car stop the Major lifted up his son and kissed him, his face, his neck and his thin arms.

"Love Zinaida Antonovna and do everything she tells you," he said.

"Who did you say?" the boy asked.

"Well—Mama ... her...."

"I love her as it is. Do you?"

Zinaida Antonovna grew pale and her whole body instinctively drew away.

"Kolya, darling," she muttered, "tell Daddy to write to you."

"Papa, you will be writing to us, won't you?"

"Yes, of course. And you write to me, Kolya. But see that you are a good, obedient boy."

"Mama will write to you and I'll draw something for you."

"Good. Well, thank you for everything.... We'll leave matters at that. Goodbye, Zinaida Antonovna," and for the first time he looked her in the eyes simply, frankly.

"But why don't you kiss Mama? You kissed me, but not Mama. Why, Papa?"

Brazhnev put his arm around her shoulders and lightly touched her forehead with his lips.

"Thank you very much, my dear, my heartfelt thanks to you."

He jumped onto a street-car and although there were plenty of empty seats in the car he stood on the step and looked back for a long time at the frail figure of the unknown woman and the frail youngster standing at her side.

Our Hands Have Grown Heavy

1

MY camel led the way salaaming right and left. Every step was a benevolent salaam. And together with it I also salaamed—to the fertile fields, the sweltering sun, the turbulent waterfalls and the majestic mountains. To our right stretched the Tien Shan range. The summits were covered with blue glaciers gleaming majestically in the rays of the sun. No, they were not a bit gloomy, but seemed to be musing sagely: they allure, beckon, hold one enraptured, as though under a spell. The foothills are covered with dark green grasses; higher up are crab apple trees, still higher—rich silver firs, and higher still —dark brown, barren peaks.

"There's plenty of game around here," said Sake, who was acting as my guide, drawing his camel alongside of mine. "Plenty of game. Wild goats, and bears, and panthers. Lots of them! And birds? Pheasants, partridges and wild ducks of all kinds and wild geese and swans. There's everything here. And plenty of them. But look— there's a thief sitting over there. I could just...."

"A thief? What can a thief be doing in the hills?"

Before Sake could reply that which he had called a thief bounded away lightly as though it were jumping over something and headed for a ravine, and by the way it was making off I guessed that it was a wolf. About a dozen or so wild goats suddenly appeared from the ravine. For an instant or so they stood stock-still and then, flourishing their white bushy tails so resembling ballet dancers, they bounded away disappearing in the hills. The wolf also stopped and, looking in our direction as though offended, made after them.

"Aha, that wolf didn't get any goats this time," Sake shouted with joy and turning to me he said heatedly: "I don't like wolves. Everything lives honestly—the wild goats, the pheasants, but the wolves are thieves and the panthers, too, are thieves. And amongst people, too, there are honest people and there are thieves. Isn't what I say true?"

"I don't know."

Sake smiled mysteriously in his oriental way.

"Thieves should be killed, isn't that so? You say that they should be taught to be different? Eh-heh! Can you teach a wolf? And there are men like them, just like wolves."

I looked searchingly at Sake, still not understanding what he was driving at. He was getting on for seventy but he sat his camel like a young man.

"What is the point you want to make, Sake?"

"Why does an honest person need a war? Tell me. Why? Well? Look around—just see what a rich region ours is. See how many crab apple trees there are? The hills are full of them. And then there are plenty of raspberry canes, and apricot and pear trees. Oh-ho-ho! And look over there—in the valley. Can your eyes see where our fields end? And in these fields of ours everything grows. Apples grow, grapes grow, wheat grows, sheep grow and cows grow Everything grows. What do I want war for? I have to work. I have a lot of work to do and then I will be wealthy, and my neighbour will be wealthy, and everybody will be wealthy. Yes, you only have to work. And that's just it—the *carapchat** wants to steal

---

* A thief in the vernacular.—*F.P.*

everything I have. He doesn't want to work. No, the *ca-rapchat* doesn't want to do that and so he must be destroyed just like a wolf," and Sake suddenly broke into his own native tongue, speaking ever so quickly, spitting and shouting just one word: "Dogs! Dogs!"

I burst out laughing.

"Sake, I can't understand what you're driving at."

Sake recollected himself:

"Yes, I was cursing, cursing furiously, cursing the fascists. The fascists—they're wolves. Isn't that so?"

Just then some pheasants—dove-coloured pheasants with flaming red feathers over their eyes—crossed our path. They were hen pheasants. They stopped and, as though at a command, they all stretched out their necks looking at us. I snatched up my rifle but Sake touched me on the arm.

"Don't shoot," he said, "they're playing."

"Do you pity them?"

"Pheasants are not thieves. You should shoot thieves...."

A flock of sheep came down the hills. Fat sheep with heavy, fat tails; they came down the slope nibbling at the young grass, overtaking one another and looking for all the world like white horses on the crests of the waves.

"Sake! Sake!" I said. "I should like to see the *chaban*. Yes, yes, I must see the shepherd."

"Shepherd? You won't see one. A shepherdess—that's possible."

"Must the *chaban* be a woman?"

"No, a man, of course. But the men have gone away, they've gone to the front. Where the husband has gone his wife has taken his place."

I turned my camel and headed for the flock of sheep. Walking in front of the flock were two women dressed in sheepskin jackets. One of them, covering her face with her hands, looked at me between her fingers. I took off my hat.

"How are you?"

"How are you, thank you, very well," they both replied at once and laughed heartily.

I could not understand the joke and glanced around at Sake. But he also was laughing.

"That's the only Russian they know," he shouted to me—"'how are you,' 'thank you,' 'very well.'"

The women continued to laugh heartily; their almond-shaped hazel eyes sparkled merrily as they rattled off something in their own tongue, pointing all the time at me.

"What are they talking about, Sake?"

"They say that you should come in the evening and be their guest of honour and they will treat you to tea, strong tea. They see that you are a military man and since that is so you are a blood brother; maybe you'll meet their husbands at the front and then you will tell them: your womenfolk are tending the sheep, guarding them from the wolves and let them, their husbands, strike out still harder at the wolves—the fascists. Oh-ho! D'you hear what our womenfolk are speaking about?!"

I made my camel kneel, got out of the saddle and walked towards the women. They stopped laughing. They suddenly became shy or so it appeared to me. But this was not so. As a matter of fact their eyes were turned in a different direction. One of them exclaimed:

"Look—the chairman!"

A horseman was galloping down the hillside sitting his saddle as though both rider and horse were one. The horse's mane fluttered in the wind. The horseman inclined slightly to one side and it seemed as though the horse flew on at will. But suddenly it stopped in its tracks, the horseman jumped out of the saddle and we saw that the rider was a woman of about forty-five with a swarthy, sun-tanned face. Striding up to me she looked me over from head to foot and blurted out angrily:

"None of your monkey business, d'you understand? Our women are good women. What are you doing here?"

158

This was so sudden that I stood there nonplussed.

"Their husbands are at the front. They're good women. What are you doing here?"

"It's Maryam Buzakarova," Sake whispered in my ear. "You were on your way to see her and now you've met."

"Maryam," I said, "I have brought you greetings from your son, from Uraz."

Maryam's stern, severe face quivered. Tears welled up in her golden, almond-shaped eyes which resembled those of her son and she stretched out her hand to me.

"Uraz! My son! Uraz! Forgive me for the bad thoughts I had in my mind," and taking both my hands she led me towards the horse. "Get onto the saddle. You should ride a horse. Get on, please and I'll take your camel."

I did as she requested.

2

She invited us to her hut. The hut was made of clay and thatched with reeds. It did not look very hospitable from the outside, the more so as we were met by an enormous pack of wolfhounds with collars studded with sharp spikes. But when we entered I was surprised how neat and cozy it was. In the front room to which Maryam led us the floor was covered with a carpet in the middle of which was a round table on short legs; to one side stood a bed on which blankets and felt covers were neatly arranged. We sat down on the carpet. Maryam gave us two cushions. Sake sat down on one

"Do the same," he whispered to me, "its the custom. The guest of honour must sit on a cushion."

I sat down. Maryam left the hut and shortly after we could hear her ringing voice in the courtyard. A fire was lit in front of the window. Two girls with long braids of hair were busying themselves around the fire. Soon after a very old man came into the room. He salaamed to us and sat down near the table. Following him came an old woman—she was small, plump and, greeting us also, sat down near the table. For some time they sat there in silence and then the old man said:

"When Uraz had scarcely turned six his father, Abilda, set him on a bareback horse and giving it a cuff with his whip sent it galloping over the steppes. Such is the custom: a man must be able to handle a horse from the age of six. And the horse bounded off in a mad gallop over the steppe, striving to throw its inexperienced rider from its back; the horse, too, does not want to submit to the rein. But young Uraz, clutching the horse's mane, hung on like a leech and when the horse, covered with foam, reached the grove, I lifted Uraz from the horse and I said at the time:

" 'You'll be a sturdy lad. A real man.'

"And Uraz replied:

" 'I know that.'

"There's a lad for you! How did he know that he would be a real man?" and the old man burst out laughing heartily, showing us a set of strong white teeth.

"He is enquiring," Sake said to me, "how is he—Uraz—getting on at the front."

"He's a real man, a sturdy man."

"There's a lad for you! I knew he would be," the old man remarked with conviction and, nodding his head to the old woman, he said to her: "Our Uraz is a sturdy man, just like your son Abilda, Uraz's father. Abilda has also left for the front—to be with his son." And the old man, with his arm around the old woman sitting next to him, began to sing—his body swaying in time with his song.

And he sang to us how he—Sabit and his young Ashe who had now grown old together with him—had begotten Abilda, a son of the steppes, a son of the mountains. And as Abilda grew up Sabit's and Ashe's bones became old. . . . "And the vitality of our bones went out to our son, to our Abilda. But we were neither angry nor envious, we were overjoyed, his mother and I, that we had such a sturdy son and that this son of ours was inheriting our strength. And then Abilda begot Uraz. . . And together with you, my old wife, we again were overjoyed that our strength was inherited by Uraz. And today both Abilda and Uraz are defending our steppes, our mountains, our peace. . . . And you and I, my old wife, can proudly hold up our heads"—and turning to me he sang: "You are our guest. You have come to us from the big city. How happy you must be because have you not seen the wisest of all men on earth. And when once again you see him say to him from me: "Far away in Kazakhstan, in the shadow of the Tien Shan Mountains, live old Sabit Buzakarov and his wife Ashe. Together they are one hundred and ninety years and they send their greetings to him—to the wisest man on earth. You'll tell him." The old man embraced me and the old woman, too, embraced me and then together they sang a song—a song that was as broad as the steppes.

The song was interrupted by the girls: they came in carrying two bowls and placed them on the table. And in one bowl was bits of boiled mutton and in the other something that resembled large pancakes, only much drier. And Maryam came into the room, blushing, looking much younger, and she placed in front of the old man the head of a sheep and an enormous pitcher of wine.

And the old man washed his hands and we also washed our hands. And he carved the meat from the bones and cut it into small pieces. And he broke the pancakes and all this he mixed together in an enormous bowl into which he poured some sauce. And then he lifted up the sheep's head. Solemnly he cut off one ear and handed it to me.

Sake said:

"Eat. You are the guest of honour."

The old man cut off the second ear and handed it to Sake.

Maryam poured out the golden wine; the girls handed us spoons. Sipping at the wine I said:

"To the health of Maryam's mother."

But everybody was silent at the table. The girls were about to take their spoons and dip them into the big bowl but the old man said something in his native tongue, looking all the time at me.

Sake whispered in my ear:

"What is in that bowl is *bish-barmak* which means—five fingers. They usually eat with their spoons but, to-day, is a red-letter day and they would very much like...."

I did not wait for Sake to finish and with my hands touched the food.... And everybody around the table was overjoyed: they stretched their hands to the bowl and took the morsels with their fingers.

Maryam sat down at my side and looking intently at me said in a whisper:

"Eat, eat. You are Uraz's friend. When you see him tell him, please: his father, too, has left for the front. And tell him also that his mother is working in the collective farm. This hand of mine," she showed me a small hand that had been roughened by the weather, "this hand of mine, although it may not be able to wield a rifle, can run our collective farm. Eat. Eat."

We fell asleep, weary from our journey, having made a hearty meal, drunk a good measure of wine and a samovar full of tea.... But in my sleep I could hear Maryam whispering not far away from me, every now and then mentioning the names of her son and her husband.

For how long I slept I do not know. Suddenly I felt somebody touch my foot.

I opened my eyes.

Maryam was there at my feet and said, looking not at me but in a different direction:

162

"My guest, my dear guest, precious to me as my own son. The people have gathered in the yard. They have come to see you."

I jumped out of bed in a flash, washed myself and went out into the yard.

The mountains loomed in the distance. The sun played on their summits and it seemed as though one mountain was moving on the other. And many people, their faces sun-tanned and swarthy, thronged the courtyard. They stood there silently and looked at me and I looked at them. And so it went on for a minute or so. The silence was broken by a woman. She shouted to me:

"Tell us about Uraz."

And I told them how one day Uraz was ordered to make his way behind the German lines and bring back a "tongue." And when dusk fell he set out. He came back the next morning his face clouded and sad. He reported:

"I crawled up to the sentry at night and hit him over the head with the butt of my rifle, caught hold of him and carried him off. But soon after I noticed that the German was dead: I had given him such a mighty blow that his helmet crushed his head."

The commander said:

"Why did you hit him so hard, you should have hit him more gently."

And Uraz replied:

"I did not intend to hit him so hard—my arms did that."

"In that case I'll have to send somebody else."

"No, no," Uraz protested. "I'll go again. This time I'll wrap some sacking around my rifle butt."

And when it grew dusk he set off again. And the next morning we saw: Uraz was back with a "tongue." He laid the "tongue" at our feet. But when we looked at the German we found that he was dead.

And we said to him:

"Uraz, the German is dead."

Uraz stood there with a look of bewilderment on his face.

"But how can that be? I did not hit him very hard. He was alive when I picked him up and carried him off. But apparently I held him so tightly that I choked the life out of him.... My hands have become heavy, Comrade Commander...."

And the hands of all our Red Armymen, just like the hands of Uraz Buzakarov, have become heavy in dealing with the enemy. Soon I shall be returning to the front. What shall I say to Uraz? What greetings shall I give him?

And the people gathered there replied without a moment's hesitation, their clenched fists—hundreds of arms —raised to the sky:

"Tell Uraz that our hands, too, have become heavy in dealing with the enemy."

But the German fascists are civilized savages and con-
scientious cannibals. Looking recently through the diaries
of German soldiers I found that one of them who, it appeared, took part in the Klin pogrom, was fond of music
and particularly "admired" Chaikovsky. Desecrating the
house of the composer that man knew what he was about.
Ravaging Novgorod the Germans wrote long-winded dis-
sertations on the "architectural beauties of Naugart"—that's
how the Germans call Novgorod.

In the pockets of one dead German our men found a
pair of baby's knickers spattered with blood and a photo-
graph of his own children. He murdered a Russian child
but his own children he undoubtedly loved. To them murder is not a manifestation of an unsound mind but a pre-
meditated act. After slaughtering thousands of children
in Kiev one Nazi wrote: "We are annihilating the offspring
of a terrible tribe...."

Of course, there are good and bad men in the ranks
of the German aggressors; but the point is not the psychic
qualities of this or that Nazi. The German "good fellows"
—those who at home give way to sentimentalities, give
pick-a-backs to the kiddies and feed the German cats
with morsels of their rationed hamburgers, murder Russian children with the same pedantry as do the bad Germans. They murder because they have come to believe
that only people with German blood are worthy of living
on this earth of ours.

At the beginning of the war I showed one Nazi war
prisoner a leaflet. This was one of the first leaflets we
published and it breathed with the naivity of a man who
had been roused from bed in the dead of night by German bombs. The leaflet stated that the Germans had made
a wanton attack on us and were conducting an unjust
war. The Hitlerite read it through and shrugged his
shoulders: "That does not interest me in the least," he
said. The question of justice did not interest him in the
least: he was out for Ukrainian pork. It had been dinned

into his ears that wars of aggression were a means of making something. He was out for "vital territory" for Germany and "booty" stockings for his wife.

What astounded us was the businesslike and efficient manner in which the Germans robbed. This was not the perniciousness of individual marauders but the flagrancy of a hoodlum soldiery—the principle on which Hitler's army is built. Every German soldier is materially interested in the robber campaign. Personally I would write a very short leaflet for the benefit of Hitler's soldiers, a leaflet containing only five words: "You won't get any pork." This is all they are capable of understanding, all that actually interests them.

In the diaries of the Germans one can find a record of what they rob; they keep an account of the chickens they gobble up and the number of blankets pilfered by them. They pillage and steal without any qualms of conscience as though it was not live people they were stripping but gooseberry bushes. If a woman refuses to hand over her baby's dress to a German soldier—he'll threaten her with his rifle. And if she dares to defend her property—he'll murder her. He does not consider it a crime: he'll as soon murder a woman as go into a forest and break twigs—without thinking twice about it.

Forced to retreat the Hitlerites consign everything to the flames: to them the Russian non-combatant population is as much an enemy as the Red Army. To leave a Russian family without a roof over their heads is considered a military achievement by them. At home, in Germany, they are forced to toe the line, they will not so much as throw a match on the floor or dare to walk on the grass in a public square. In our country they have trampled underfoot entire regions, defiled entire cities, turned museums into latrines and converted schools into stables. This is done not only by clodhoppers from Pomerania or herdsmen from the Tyrol, it is being done by assistant professors, writers, "doctors of philosophy," and "learned counsels" reared by Hitler.

When our Red Armymen—our collective farmers of yesterday—saw for the first time, in the Moscow or Tula regions, entire villages in which only the chimney stacks and dove-cots had remained, they thought of their own villages on the Volga or in Siberia. They saw women and children exposed to the bitter frosts, robbed by the Germans of every bit of clothing. And a savage hatred gripped hold of them.

One German general, ordering his subordinates to show no mercy to the civilian population, added: "Sow fear in their midst." Fools and dolts—they do not understand the Russian nature. They sowed not fear but the wind that will reap the storm. The first scaffold set up by the Germans on Soviet soil made many things clear.

Now everybody in our country knows that this war does not in any way resemble the wars that went before it. For the first time our people have found pitted against them not human beings but vile, malicious monsters, savages, armed with everything that modern science can give, fiends who act according to rules and regulations and refer to science, for whom the slaughter of infants in arms is the last word of statecraft.

Hate did not come to us easily. Entire cities and regions, hundreds of thousands of human lives—this was the price we paid for it. But now our hatred is ripe, it no longer goes to the head like young wine, it has become cold and deliberate. We have realized that the world is too small a place to hold both us and the fascists. We have realized that there can be no question of compromise or coming to terms, that the question at issue is plain and simple: our right to exist.

And having learnt to hate, our people have not lost the good inherent in them. Need one mention that what they have been through has quickened their hearts. One cannot think without emotion of the mothers of large families who, in our trying times, are adopting orphans and sharing their last with them.

I recall to mind young Lyuba Sossunkevich, a military feldsher. Under enemy fire she rendered first aid to the wounded. The dugout was surrounded by Germans. Revolver in hand she fought single-handed against a dozen German soldiers, defended the wounded men under her charge and saved them from the inhuman treatment and torture that would have been their lot.

Or take the modest work of another Russian girl— Varya Smirnova—who under rifle and trench mortar gun fire delivers letters to the very front lines, guarding them as something most precious. She said to me: "It's only natural ... after all everybody's so anxious to get a letter. Life would be so dismal without letters from home...."

But the Russians do not evince a deep concern only for their own people. They understand the sufferings of other people, too. What profound human sympathy emanates from the declaration of the women of much-suffering Leningrad to the women of London. How many times have the Red Armymen questioned me about the sufferings of desecrated Paris. I happened to be present once when the Red Armymen were listening to a newspaper report telling how the Nazis had doomed the people of Greece to death from starvation, and one of the men, a collective farmer from Saratov Region, said: "It's a real calamity.... Everywhere it's the same. We've got to wipe out those Fritzes as quickly as possible so as to help people."

Our hatred for the Hitlerites is dictated by love—love of our country, love for man, love for humanity. And in this is the force of our hatred. In this is its justification. Coming to grips with the Hitlerites we see how blind hatred has destroyed Germany's soul. We are far from such hatred. We hate each and every Hitlerite because he is a representative of a misanthropic principle, because he is a convinced murderer, a robber on principle, we hate every one of them for everything they have singly and jointly done in our country and in other countries, for the tears of the widows, for the blighted children's lives, for the dreary caravans of refugees, for the fields trampled underfoot, for the millions of lives and the fruits of long years of highly creative labour they have destroyed.

We are fighting not against human beings, but against robots who resemble human beings but do not have a grain of humanism in them. Our hatred is so much stronger because in appearance they look like human beings, because they can laugh, because they can pat a horse or a dog, because in their diaries they indulge in introspection and because they have taken on the guise of human beings and civilized Europeans.

We often use words changing their original meaning. It is not of base hatred that our people dream in calling for vengeance. It is not for this that we brought up our boys and girls that they should stoop to the level of the atrocities perpetrated by the Nazis. Never will our Red Armymen murder German children, set fire to Goethe's house in Weimar or to the libraries in Marburg. Vengeance—that means paying one back in one's own kind, to speak to one in one's own tongue. But we do not have a common tongue with the fascists.

What we are yearning for is not vengeance but justice. We are out to destroy the Hitlerites so that the principles of humanity shall again flourish on the earth. We rejoice at life in all its variegated and intricate forms and aspects, the native traits of nations and people. There is sufficient room for everybody on this earth of ours. And the German people, too, shall live, having purged themselves of the monstrous crimes of the Hitler decade. But even the widest latitudes have their boundaries: just now I do not want to think or speak about the future happiness of a Germany rid of Hitler—such thoughts and words would be out of place and insincere as long as millions of Hitlerites are running amok on our soil.

Iron exposed to bitter frost sears like fire. The antithesis of hatred is life-giving love. "Death to the German aggressors"—these words sound like a vow, like an oath of allegiance to life. The Red Armymen who are meting out death to the Hitlerites do not stint their lives. What inspires them is a magnanimous integral feeling and who can say where incense against the ruthless enemy ends and the ties of blood which bind one to one's country begins. The death of every Nazi evokes a sigh of relief on the part of millions of people. The death of every Nazi is a pledge that the children of the Volga region will know no sorrow and that the ancient liberties of Paris will again be reinstated. The death of every Nazi is the elixir that will save the world.

A Christian legend tells how St. George slayed the dragon in order to liberate the fair prisoner. Today the Red Army is slaying the Nazis in order to bring liberty to harassed mankind. The struggle is stern, the task is no easy one, but no task can be loftier than this.